THE DUKE'S HELLION

Duke Dare, Book 3

Eliana Piers

Dragonblade Publishing, Inc. is an imprint of Kathryn Le Veque Novels, Inc.
P.O. Box 23
Moreno Valley, CA 92556
ceo@dragonbladepublishing.com

Produced in the United States of America

First Edition July 2025
Trade Paperback Edition

ARE YOU SIGNED UP FOR DRAGONBLADE'S BLOG?

You'll get the latest news and information on exclusive giveaways, exclusive excerpts, coming releases, sales, free books, cover reveals and more.

Check out our complete list of authors, too!

No spam, no junk. That's a promise!

Sign Up Here

www.dragonbladepublishing.com

Dearest Reader;

Thank you for your support of a small press. At Dragonblade Publishing, we strive to bring you the highest quality Historical Romance from some of the best authors in the business. Without your support, there is no 'us', so we sincerely hope you adore these stories and find some new favorite authors along the way.

Happy Reading!

CEO, Dragonblade Publishing

Additional Dragonblade books by Author Eliana Piers

Duke Dare Series
The Duke's Spinster (Book 1)
The Duke's Goddess (Book 2)
The Duke's Hellion (Book 3)

CHAPTER ONE

1816 England

SOMETIMES YOU GET exactly what you want out of life and love. Sometimes the most perfect plan, the most daring dream, and the most impossible fantasy…they all come true.

Not often.

But sometimes.

And if that most perfect plan, most daring dream, most impossible fantasy were to come true for Artemisia, she wasn't even sure how she would pinpoint it.

There were so many options to choose from. First, and often foremost, there was the rescue of a highwayman. She would have been traveling to visit her aunt. No, her sister. Or maybe her friend—never mind, that part didn't matter. She was in a carriage. An enclosed space. At the mercy of her driver and anyone reckless enough to lay siege. And someone always did in this fantasy.

The shout would come, *Stand and deliver.* The door would be kicked in. She would scream. Not helplessly of course, that wasn't her style. She would yell something fierce, like, *You picked the wrong carriage.* Or something equally bold, such as, *This isn't going to end well for you.* Wait, better, *And you thought this was going to be your lucky day? Think again.* Yes, something outstanding like that.

The highwayman would drag her out of the carriage, gruffly (but not too disrespectfully) and he would hold her back to his chest. She would feel his whole body against hers (even though she had no idea what that really felt like), but simply imagining it was enough to make her body shudder with desire. He would smell faintly like whiskey, but of course he wasn't a drunk. That would be too slovenly for her tastes. And his clothes would be rough against her untouched skin.

The highwayman cared nothing for his fellow man. He shot for the kill. He lived for pleasure. He existed for himself. But he would see something in her. She was different. She was the one he had been waiting for but didn't even know he hadn't been intaking oxygen until he met her. So even though he handled her roughly, he did it with intent.

Then he would whisper in her ear. *Don't think I won't take* everything *from you. Everything.* As in, her body, in case that wasn't clear. But it was always clear because at that point her nipples would be cutting slits in her dress begging to be released, and she would reply with, *You can take it if you want.*

Yes, that was a good contender for the ultimate fantasy.

But if not the highwayman, likely it would be the pirate. The rogue of a man with long dark hair blowing in the wind, standing aboard his ship, eyeing her. And only her. He would tilt his head, acknowledging her, inviting her to come aboard. No. That was all wrong. He would spot her across the room of a crowded tavern and haul her out on his shoulder in front of everyone. She would struggle. All for show of course. And then he would probably swat her bottom, but that wouldn't stop her from kicking him. And she would scream and kick all the way aboard his ship and into his captain's cabin where he would fling the door open and kick it shut with his foot. Then he would pin her against the wall and with smoldering eyes he would lean in with his plush lips and hard body, and—

"Mimi, isn't this the store you wanted to visit?" her sister Zenobia asked, placing a gentle hand on her arm, stopping them in front of a red door facing the street.

Drat. Another fantasy cut short due to the beckoning of reality. If only she could be left uninterrupted for a few hours. A day. A week might do.

"Yes, thank you. This is it, Nobi." It was a distracted reply. She was still woolgathering about the bulge in the pirate's breeches that was being pressed up against her—

"Was it the knight this time?"

"Huh? Nighttime?"

Nobi nudged her with her elbow. "Knight or pirate?" she asked with a wink.

"Mmm. Yes. Pirate," Mimi wiggled her eyebrows. "You know me too well."

"That I do." Nobi sighed, "Plus, you've been more distracted lately. Ever since Joan got engaged. The duke dare has been on your mind, hasn't it?"

"I don't want to think about it."

"Doesn't mean it hasn't been on your mind," Nobi prodded.

"True. But all the same, I don't feel like talking about it right now."

"You do remember that you were the one who initiated it, right?"

"Was I though?"

"Yes."

Mimi dismissed the argument with a wave of her hands. "I still don't want to talk about it."

"Because you're next?"

Mimi pursed her lips.

"And because you're upset with me?"

Mimi shrugged. Her sister knew her *far* too well. It was distressing how well Nobi could read her. There was no hiding anything.

"I know you're not ready to take your turn, Nobi." Mimi exhaled roughly, empathizing with the turmoil her sister was feeling. "I just wish you were."

"Me too"—Nobi shook her head and a few dark tresses slid out of her coiffure to frame her face—"I wish I was ready, too."

The ache in Nobi's voice and the tremor in her shoulders rocked through Mimi. She may be harsh at times, but she wasn't completely calloused, so she wrapped her arm around her older sister. "I understand. You have to do it in your time. And we're all here for you." And then to add some levity, she said, "Well, at least I am. Bodi and Joan may be a bit busy now, what with their new husbands and betrotheds and all. So you have me. For better or worse. And one day soon we shall both be saying those words to the loves of our lives."

"I hope so." The weariness in Nobi's voice was not lost on Mimi.

"I know so. Trust me." She pulled Nobi's hand and opened the red door. "Now, let's shop."

It was an archery store, and the second Mimi entered it, she felt as though she had stepped into one of her very own fantasies. Bows of all kinds and sizes lined the walls. Arrows with varying arrowheads. Quivers of all colors and materials. This was a dream come true. Since the pirate was not here, at least *this*, she would take.

It took Mimi a moment to find her bearings. It was almost too much to take in at once. But as her eyes adjusted to the marvels before her, she slowly turned around.

And then her pupils surely dilated. All her dreams *were* coming true. Never in her life had she seen anything so perfect. Dark tan in color. Tall in length. Strong. Sturdy. Solid and thick enough to carry a full load. Could carry her load. That's the one.

The golden quiver.

"Nobi," Mimi spoke softly so as not to disturb the magical item.

"Yes?"

"Shh!"

"Why are we whispering?"

"Look." Mimi pointed. That should satisfy Nobi's question.

"What am I looking at?"

Apparently it did not satisfy her.

"The golden quiver," Mimi said in reverence. "It's the most incredible, singular piece of equipment I've ever seen."

Nobi raised her brows in response and gestured toward the quiver. "That?"

Mimi struck her sister's hand down. "Don't point at it."

"What are talk—"

"Shh. Don't talk. Just let me be alone with it."

"Oh my God, Mimi. You are so dramatic sometimes."

Mimi didn't respond. She couldn't because it was one hundred percent true. But also, she had no inclination to respond because all she wanted was silence with the beauty before her.

"I'll be browsing the book section, Mimi. Take your time. I know you've been looking forward to this." With a pat on her arm, Nobi took off, leaving Mimi to stare.

Her eyes rested on the magnificent specimen of equipment. She could imagine herself wearing it already. And in her mind she was glorious. Lightweight. Accessible. Everything she could ask for.

And just as she reached out her hand to encircle the quiver of her dreams, a thicker, manlier, somewhat hairier hand beat her to it.

"Excuse me," the voice reverberated.

And she looked up into a golden face framed with golden hair. The likes of which matched the golden quiver.

His hand brushed hers as he clasped the quiver and took it under his arm.

And Mimi, of all the women to have this happen to, was speechless. Perhaps for the first time in her life.

What was happening right now? Her dreams were crashing, colliding, intermingling. When still she said nothing, the man spoke, "I've been looking for this one. If you don't mind."

And her eyes followed him to the counter where he paid for the quiver. *Her* quiver. The quiver that made her liver quiver.

She cleared her throat. "Excuse me, I was about to buy that."

The man furrowed his brow, "I don't think so. You're a wom—"

"I'm an archer," she finished for him before he could insult her.

"Well, I suppose you'll get the next one then." He had hardly taken the time to take a brief glimpse of her.

"Your Grace," the clerk started, "shall I wrap this up for you?"

"Thank you." With that, his attention had already moved on from her.

Her heart was pounding against her ribcage while her feet were locked in place. Her hands were fisted at her sides, but light was cascading into the store illuminating the duke. And she suddenly knew what this was. She knew what was happening. It wasn't just about the quiver. It was about a man.

Fate.

It made no sense, but it was fate. There were moments in life where fate boomed its voice and spoke clearly. When it shouted down from Heaven pointing the way of the future. This was such a time as that.

"Mimi?" For the second time that morning, Nobi nudged her sister with her elbow and whispered, "Are you all right? You're staring."

"Who is that?" There was only one other person in the store, the duke, so Mimi needn't clarify the question she posed to her sister.

"The Duke of Vanic?" Nobi supplied the name she'd been waiting to hear. Eager to know the man, the duke, a fellow archer.

In hushed tones, Mimi repeated the name, "The Duke of Vanic. It's fate, Nobi."

"What's fate?"

Standing awkwardly in the middle of the store staring, the two sisters would have appeared peculiar to anyone else, but not to the Duke of Vanic. Mostly because he didn't bother with a second glance.

But Mimi paid that no mind.

"It's fate to have met him here." She heaved out a long sigh. "And now." She unclenched her fists and pulled her hands up to her heart. "He's my duke dare."

Nobi blew a soft sound from her lips. "You don't even know him, Mimi."

"I know him enough. Sometimes it's enough to trust fate. He walked into my life and took my dreams. But it's all a sign. *He* is my dream. Not the quiver, but the man. It's an analogy, no? He's the quiver in which rests all my fantasies."

"So you're not upset about the actual quiver?" Nobi gestured toward the empty space where the quiver had once been on display.

"What quiver?"

"The golden one. The most incredible one—"

"Pfft. No. I mean, yes. It was—is—incredible. But I have a more important mission now."

"What's that?" Nobi picked up an arrowhead and was flipping it back and forth between her palms.

"He's the one. The duke for me. I can feel it. Something is about to happen, and he is it."

Nobi rubbed her shoulder gently. "He hardly looked at you, Mimi. I'm not certain he would recognize you if he saw you again."

Undeterred, Mimi straightened her shoulders. "It doesn't matter. It's up to me to secure his attention. This was a dare after all. Now I have the challenge ahead of me. I can see it so clearly." She rubbed her hands together. "This is what the duke dare was all about, Nobi. And you know it." Mimi reached her hand, palm extended, out into the open air. "The intention was to set your sights on what you wanted and to go after it." She clenched her hand together forcefully, grasping the empty air. "I'm about to show you how it's done. You know how much I love a challenge."

"Really, Mimi. You should have gone into theater."

"It's not too late," Mimi chuckled.

"It may not be too late, but it's far too scandalous." Nobi shook her head. "I should love for you to show your older sister how to play the game of love."

"Don't you worry. As sharp a shooter as you are, and as accurate an archer as I am, I shall take my aim and I shall not miss."

Nobi just shrugged. Which, in and of itself should have been considered an innocent gesture, but to Mimi, no, it was not innocent. It was a challenge.

"You don't think I can snag him?"

Nobi placed her hands on Mimi's shoulders. "My dear, *younger* sister, you don't even know him. How can you think you're in love with him?"

And even though she hadn't said the words, she realized that that was exactly what she had been conveying. Being instantly struck by cupid's arrow. Smitten. Besotted. Yes, that sounded right. That's how fate always worked, no?

"Cupid's arrow doesn't miss. Don't you remember Joan and James?" It didn't seem real that Mimi needed to remind her own sister of the role they had played in Joan and James finding love with each other.

"Of course, but that was completely different."

"Not even one bit. Mark my words. Cupid's arrow has struck. Love will abound. It's fate. And fate has never led me astray before. Not even once."

CHAPTER TWO

S AM, THE DUKE of Cadmore, sat in front of the fireplace waiting for his butler to enter. His jaw clenched so tightly it produced an erratic tick. Chris sat across from him, drumming his fingers lightly on the arm of his chair.

"Are you going to tell me why I'm here? Usually we frequent White's, not your drawing room."

"What I have to do, I'd rather not do publicly." Sam scrubbed his hand down his face. If there were another option, he would like to consider it. But he trusted Chris. This was best. Even if he had to keep reminding himself of it, he would go through with this.

"Mysterious, is it?" Chris chuckled, unaware of the heaviness that would soon befall him.

"You could say that…" Sam let the sentence hang in the air, hoping it would sufficiently fill the silence he craved for a few more moments.

"Can you at least tell me why there's a fire going in the middle of summer?" It was asked with a smirk, but Sam didn't notice.

"I felt cold." True. He felt cold. But not just his body. Something in his soul felt as though it were frosting over, whether for protection or for another reason, he wasn't sure. He could only hope that this was the right decision.

"Your Grace," the butler said when he entered the room with a small box in his hands. Making his way to the two friends, he stood stoically, awaiting a reply.

"Bixly. About time. Just place it on the table in front of the Duke of Saxby. Leave it closed and go. That will be all."

"As you wish," Bixly murmured blandly, doing precisely what his master instructed. Bixly was loyal to a fault. It's been said that every man has his price, but not Bixly. He held his duties in his mind with the highest honor, grace, and dignity. His family had been serving Sam's family for generations, and there was no end in sight.

Once Bixly had exited the room, Chris raised his brows and asked, "What's this?"

"You know what it is." He couldn't bring himself to say it. And he knew that Chris was intelligent enough to figure it out.

Chris's eyebrows reached for the ceiling. "Really? Here? Why now?"

"My cousin is coming for a visit, and I don't want him anywhere near them."

"Rudolph?"

"The one and only," Sam said in a way that indicated his disdain for his blood relative. It was a wonder the two were related. Then again, familial relations often provided quite the disparity in personalities and values amongst its own. And no two could be further from each other than Sam and Rudolph, who was next in line for the dukedom.

"Hmm…I can see your reasoning. But won't you be here with him?"

"Sadly, no. Sally and Jacob are getting married, and they've invited everyone to a house party before the wedding."

"And you're going?"

"James insists we go. He claims he's the mastermind behind the two getting together."

"I heard it was Joan?"

"It probably was," Sam said and the two laughed. It felt good to relieve some of the tension in his face. He could still feel his clenched jaw, but it wasn't ticking anymore. "Either way, I'm attending the house party, which means Rudolph will have too much time here all by himself. I don't trust him."

"So you want me to take these?" Chris pointed to the wooden box. The action was just as intense as Sam would want. He knew he had chosen the right man for the job.

"Guard them with your life. I know you have the safest place for them."

Chris nodded solemnly, not asking the question that Sam knew he wanted to pose. Sam answered it for him anyway, "I can't relinquish them to Wes yet."

"Understood."

"I know I lost the bet, but…something doesn't feel right. I have to sort it out before I can pay up."

"He doesn't care."

Sam let his head fall into his hands. "It doesn't matter. I made the bet and lost. I owe him."

"He wouldn't make you pay up."

"I'm an honorable man, Chris." Sam could feel the heat racing from his heart center all the way through his limbs. "Even if I would never duel, I have my honor."

"I never questioned it." Chris's voice was placating, as though speaking with a raging bear.

And in a second, Sam might get there, to be the raging bear that is. But, no, he wouldn't. Not today. Not ever, if he could help it. He knew the stakes. He knew what it meant to keep himself in check and manage his emotions. He would not accept the fate of his father. If nothing else in life, Sam would not live like him.

It was just another way he competed. He made himself the polar opposite of his father. Always in control. Always reaching for his best. And more often than not attaining it.

When Chris spoke, it stirred Sam to realize that they had been sitting in silence. "I can't believe that bastard is coming here."

"He doesn't know that I suspect anything."

Chris scoffed. "He is truly that unaware? He doesn't know

that you suspect him of wanting to kill you? He thinks he is that discreet? You must be joking."

"Unless he's a better actor than most, he knows nothing. He thinks we're on friendly terms. I know it's hard to believe, but I don't want him to know that I know."

"For obvious reasons."

"Exactly." Sam brought two fingers to his cheek and held his jaw up with his thumb. His lips rested against the knuckle of his fourth finger. If there was a way to think long enough and hard enough to predict the future, he would be attempting to do so now.

"Why is he coming here?" That was precisely the question Sam wanted to answer in his attempts to be a seer.

"I wish I knew. He says he wants to visit." Chris laughed knowingly and Sam continued. "We both know that's a lie. But I can't figure out why he would be here now, other than to make another attempt on my life."

"Perhaps it's best that you do attend the house party."

Sam nodded in agreement. "At the very least, it buys me time to secure more protection."

"That shouldn't be too hard."

"It's always a challenge to know who to trust. I can pay several men to protect me, but if even one leaks out some information, even unwittingly, that could be it."

"At least you have Bixly."

"That's true. I can always trust him."

"Why bother with letting Rudolph stay at your place at all then?"

"I don't want him to know that I'm onto him. At this stage, I think I have the advantage, but I can't be sure. If I reject him, or avoid him, I might give myself away."

"True…" Chris mirrored the thinking pose that Sam still held. "What's the plan?"

"Right now the plan is to attend the house party and draw it out for as long as possible. Secondary to that, I'll surround myself with people I trust. And I'll avoid Rudolph as much as I think I can without it being noticeable. The rest I'll have to figure out as I go."

"Is there anything else I should know?"

The answer to that question felt almost ridiculous to say aloud. That a man should fear his cousin. A power-hungry, money-seeking, status-hunting lout. But he wasn't the only man in the history of the world who had ever been on his guard around family. Sadly, it was a more common occurrence than it should be. Taking a deep breath, he said the words aloud, "All I know is that he is up to something. I don't know what it could be other than to obtain the dukedom for himself."

Without flinching, Chris asked, "What are we going to do about it?"

And that right there, that one word—*we*—that was enough to let Sam breathe a sigh of relief.

He wasn't in this alone. That's all he needed to know for now.

"When I know, you'll know."

"All right. Well, this is one less thing you have to worry about, Sam." Chris stood, taking the box under one arm. He slapped Sam on the shoulder. "I've got this. You worry about the rest."

Despite not being a very physically affectionate man, he couldn't stop himself from standing and giving Chris a quick embrace.

"Thank you."

When the two separated, Chris waved and exited the room, leaving Sam alone to ponder everything. It was exactly where he thought he wanted to be, except now that he was here, the contemplations were more abundant than he expected.

Rudolph would arrive in a couple of days. Sam would already be gone. He had briefed his servants on how to handle his cousin, and so long as he could trust them, which he was fairly certain of, everything should work out fine. So really, all he needed to worry about was the upcoming house party.

There, he would be surrounded with people he liked. For the most part. Really, there was only one person he wasn't too eager to see. But surely she would fade into the background. Who was he kidding? She was not the fading type. In fact, she might be the least fading type that he knew. That was part of the reason he wasn't too eager to see her.

Fade? No. Display? Dissect? Dramatize? Yes, yes, and yes. If she caught wind of anything going on, she would be the one to interrogate everyone until she found what she was looking for. Even if she had no clue what she was really looking for.

Sam shuddered. All the more reason to maintain his status quo and keep his secrets. No sense in letting her see anything—even a small thing—was off. It was easy enough to stay away from her…well, that wasn't true. Chris was going and Nobi was going. And since Mimi would be attached to Nobi's hip, and Sam would be attached to Chris's hip…well, the four would definitely be in community.

Sam scrubbed his face again. Perhaps the house party wasn't the best idea. But he had already accepted the invitation, and if anything, he was a man of his word.

As long as their host, Sally, organized a few activities. Challenges. He should be all right. A challenge. That's exactly what he needed. If he could sink his teeth into a challenge that would keep him distracted and would give him purpose.

It was settled. And really, it was quite simple. That's all Sam ever needed. A challenge.

CHAPTER THREE

S AM ARRIVED AT the house party early that Saturday morning with Chris in tow. The two had planned to arrive together, mostly for Sam's sanity. Sam assumed Chris was being a good friend and helping him out. If he had other motives, well, Sam could guess at what (or who) that might entail, but he pretended to let the man have his secrets.

"Do you think we'll see much of James at this house party?" Chris asked as the two men found comfortable spots to have a quiet drink.

Sam scoffed at the question. "Doubtful. The man is head over ears in love with Joan. Pfft. With their recent engagement, we'll be lucky to see them for meals. That man will be sequestering that woman every chance he gets."

"Of course, you're right. And I don't think she'll be fighting him on that at all. What with the way she looks at him." Chris's hands rubbed the sides of his armchair before he added, "I'd be the same way with a woman."

"I, for one, would not."

Chris laughed. "Every man says that until he meets the love of his life."

"First of all, not every man says that."

"Only the self-proclaimed bachelors then?" Chris supplied as a replacement.

"Yes, better. But second of all, that's quite the statement to make."

"What? That she's the love of his life?"

"Yes."

"Well, she is, isn't she?" Chris queried.

"I suppose…if you must call it that."

"I must. If James can believe in love, anyone can."

Sam merely shrugged his shoulders in reply. It was true. James claimed to not believe in the existence of love, and then—poof—Joan, and the man was transformed.

"In fact, he doesn't just believe in it, he found it."

"Rather quickly, no?"

"Are you saying you question its authenticity?" Unflappable Chris gave him a side look.

"Not at all."

"Good. His love happened quickly. Love can be like that. It isn't always that way. Some love burns slowly. Takes time to build, catch, and blaze its path."

"God, you're speaking as if from experience." Sam eyed his friend. Surely the words coming out of his mouth were not mere conjecture, but this time it was Chris who gave the noncommittal reply. He didn't see much point in prying for further information, knowing Chris would share in his own time. "It's a good thing we chose to come early as we have a chance to relax before the chaos of guests starts."

Chris nodded along distractedly, already lost in his thoughts. Probably about some slow-burning love that Sam knew next to nothing about. He had an inkling…but…he wasn't sure, so he allowed himself the pleasure of being in his own thoughts.

Being early meant Sam could get comfortable, surveille his surroundings, and take the offensive with newly arriving guests. Though it should be noted that the offensive he took looked rather more like a defensive... since he (and Chris) were essentially in hiding.

Unfortunately his hiding place—that of the library—was quickly discovered. No sooner had he closed his eyes to permit contemplation(or a short nap), than an interruption in the form of two ladies appeared.

Mimi and Nobi walked into the library unaware that he and Chris had already laid claim to the space. True, it was quite a large space, and two people really couldn't claim its entirety. But they certainly made a valiant attempt.

"Oh," Mimi scowled at him. Expected. "It's you."

"It is I." Something about her caused an upset stomach, and he couldn't help mocking her. "And that is you."

Mimi crossed her arms. "What are you doing here?"

A scolding hiss flew from Nobi's lips, "Mimi!" Meanwhile Chris's shoulders shook in what Sam could only assume to be mirth.

Since Chris's head was in a book, Sam was the one to reply. "We're reading. I assume you have come to do the same thing."

"As a matter of fact, we're on our way to do some archery." She tugged on Nobi's arm before her sister could reach up and grab one of the books she was eyeing nearest to her. "We were just on our way out." Mimi spoke matter-of-factly despite everyone's awareness of the detour through the house they would have had to take if they were actually about to partake in archery activities.

What a silly chit to resent him so much that she would tell such a bounder.

*Though…archery…*he pondered, tapping his chin. That did sound tremendously more diverting than reading a book when it was such a nice day. As much as he enjoyed reading, he much preferred any and all competitive activities.

Chris sat next to him flipping the pages of his book. He didn't seem all that interested in the conversation. Then again, now that Sam studied his friend's movements, Chris was flipping those pages a little too quickly to be reading and comprehending any text his eyes might be perceiving. Every so often Chris's eye wandered up and over the edge of the page and caught a glimpse of Nobi.

Well. There was always that.

Sam needed the challenge provided by an archery activity, and Chris needed…whatever that was about. Ignoring Chris's possible reactions, and with his mind made up, Sam stood and announced, "We'll join you."

Chris dropped his book. Nobi fumbled with the spine she was tracing. Mimi, the statue, didn't wince.

With a glare, she replied, "You weren't invited."

A second chastising from Nobi permeated the air, "Mimi, really!"

"That's all right. We'll join you anyway. We could use the activity. Come." Sam grabbed Chris by his bicep and pulled him to standing. "Let's go."

After sneaking another glance at Nobi, Chris shrugged his shoulders. The four of them exited the room and made their way to the targets.

"I trust you know where they are and we're not blindly following you to nowhere?" Sam asked Mimi.

After a contemptible harrumph, Mimi answered, "Of course I know where I'm going—"

"It's just that your first attempt led you to the library."

"Yes, well, everyone makes mistakes sometimes. Life is about moving past them." She stated with such a glare that Sam couldn't help laughing. On the inside. He didn't yet want to disclose the fact that she could make him laugh, despite their numerous previous encounters in which she did exactly that.

"Are you sure this is a good idea?" Chris whispered beside him as Mimi stormed ahead.

"Competition is always a good idea." Sam swept Chris's hand off his shoulder. "Besides, I love a challenge."

"I know." Chris replaced his hand on Sam's shoulder but with a firmer grip this time. "But are you sure you want the challenge of her?"

"This isn't about her."

"Right."

Sam scoffed. "This is about the archery, my good man. I'm about to win at something."

"Are you in the right frame of mind to do this? Right now? With her?" Chris canted his head to the lithe blue-eyed blonde sashaying her hips to the targets. Not that Sam noticed all of those attributes. Consciously.

"I'm always in the right frame of mind. You would think you would know that about me. I'm not James. I'm not reckless." He spat out the words. Even though he loved his friends—yes, he was comfortable with the word love—he was honest enough to label them for what they were when needed. And for some reason Chris was confusing him with James. Sam was competitive. Not impulsive. He wasn't the kind to jump the seven-foot stile to prove a point when everyone else rode around it.

But he was always the kind to pick up a weapon, aim, and release. And he was usually the kind to win.

And there was nothing akin to the feeling of winning. Of being his best. Though he didn't feel his best at the moment, there was nothing stopping him from achieving that. He only needed to focus his thoughts. Remove the distraction of Chris in his ear and Mimi in his eye.

"Are we doing this?" Sam shouted, intentionally moving quickly toward Mimi. From the corner of his eye he saw Chris shake his head, and he was pretty sure he heard a whisper from Nobi.

"It'll be all right," or something equally reassuring.

And yes, it would be all right. Nothing was going to happen. It was a simple game—competition.

Nothing could go wrong.

Only a few moments later, Sam was taking aim, focusing on the target thirty paces away. He should be able to hit this. It was easy. He just needed to breathe. A deep inhalation only confused him. Vanilla and sugar infused itself in his nostrils. That was not the scent a man needed when he was concentrating. Then again, a man also didn't need the worry of a threat on his life or livelihood taking up residence in the back of his mind either. If a thought was going to take up space, it should at least do some farming, be productive, and pay its way. No, not these thoughts today. Rudolph and Mimi, equally aggravating but in the most polar opposite of ways.

He huffed out a breath and released the bow.

Dash it. He hit the very perimeter of the target.

"Nice shot," Mimi teased. And what he wouldn't give to…what…he was grasping at straws. What did he want to do to her? Nothing drastic…just shut her up. The only way to do that was to beat her.

"I have another shot," he ground out.

"You'll need it," she rejoined with pursed lips. And as he set up his next arrow, she had the audacity to call out to Nobi and Chris. Loudly. "Aren't you two joining us?"

"No, we have decided to sit this round out," Nobi answered at a more respectful decibel than her sister.

Sam stole a quick glance over to Nobi and Chris huddled together, whispering at the outskirts of the field. They weren't touching, but he could see Chris leaning in. What was it about those two? They were old friends, yet there was always a peculiar tension between them. Sam shook it off. He didn't have the patience to consider his friend's problems. He had enough of his own that he was trying to avoid. And he wasn't even sure his thinking was logical at this point. All he knew was that he needed to hit the target. He needed a win. Right. Now.

He took aim. Lifted his elbow. Pulled back on the bow. Narrowed his gaze. Release.

Zing!

Thunk!

The beastly arrow missed the bullseye again. By far too much.

"Bah!" Mimi couldn't suppress the sound. Or so he assumed noticing her hand covering her mouth. She withdrew her fingers and said, "I thought you would be a challenge for me."

Apparently she hadn't been trying to suppress anything. The blasted chit said whatever was on her mind. And Sam, not usually an angry fellow, felt right furious in the moment.

With gritted teeth, he formed a few polite words. As many as he could muster. "Let's see you try."

Mimi laughed. "I could do better blindfolded."

"I doubt it."

With a toss of her hair, Mimi called back to Nobi. "Do you think I could do better than that if I were blindfolded?"

The helpless shrug of Nobi's shoulders and her pitying eyebrows said it all.

"I'll go retrieve my arrows and you can take your turn."

"Don't bother. They're not in my way," she tossed out and flicked him an annoying little grin.

"Just shoot," Sam ground out.

Mimi took aim.

Bullseye!

Without a pause, she withdrew a second arrow. Load. Aim. Shoot.

Bullseye!

The smirk on her face when she turned to face him boiled his blood. Her eyes were closed. "I only closed my eyes, it's not as though I doubled the distance. I didn't want to humiliate you completely."

"Ha ha."

"Oh. You don't believe me?" Mimi stood with a hand on her hip.

Wait. Was she actually claiming that she took those shots with both of her eyes closed? Her depth perception, balance, and everything would be skewed. It was impossible. No. She wasn't saying that. She couldn't be saying that. She couldn't be that much better than him. Well, him at his worst, really. But still. A no-eyed woman was a better archer than him? It couldn't be.

"Duke," she nearly shouted, and he could hear the venom in her voice. "Are you calling me a liar?"

Speechless. That's all that he was. What should he say to that? Prove it?

"Shall I prove it?"

Thank God she supplied the words for him.

"Stand here." She motioned for him to stand beside her while she took aim again, lifted her bow and stretched it taut. Her body was preternaturally still, holding the shape of her shot. Closing her eyes, she let the arrow fly.

For a moment, Sam couldn't take his eyes off of her. She was a hellion to be sure. Wild. Furious. Even reckless, perhaps. But when he slid his eyes over to the target, without much motivation if he was being transparent, he saw what he was loath to imagine.

Bullseye. Times two.

Damn it.

"There's something off about you today," she said as though what she just did wasn't the most impressive thing in archery he had ever seen. Mimi eyed him from toe to head. The perusal made him quite uncomfortable. What was she looking at? Worse. What was she looking for?

Argh. He knew she would be the kind to notice the smallest anomaly.

Though, really, his aim was not the *smallest* anomaly. They were actually quite obvious anomalies. Why had he agreed to this challenge again? Right. He needed a distraction. Well, this was as good as it was going to get right now.

With a scowl, he said, "If you beat me at my worst, it's nothing."

"Of course you would say that because I won."

"You really think I was on top of my game just now?" he growled.

"I can't picture you on top of anything right now."

And oh, he could picture himself atop many things at the moment, but that was really veering toward dangerous ground.

"You think that right there was a display of my best?"

She scrunched her nose and conceded with a murmur, "Doubtful."

"Exactly. And that's why I'm grumbling. But I will say this, if you do beat me at my best, I'll celebrate for you." He had celebrated a woman's triumph over him before, he could do it again. Surely. Even if it meant celebrating *her*.

"I'll believe that when I see it."

"And I'll do it when you actually beat me."

Harrumphs expelled from both of them. And they stormed off to retrieve their arrows.

CHAPTER FOUR

W HAT A SORE loser. Couldn't the man just fake a smile and congratulate her? Ladies of society were basically walking in masked smiles all day every day, surely he could produce one for a second. Then again, she knew the win wasn't really worth it. Something was definitely off with Sam. He was not the grumbling type. Competitive. Fierce in his own way. Sure. But not angry or bitter.

She should have let him win. Bah! That was a terrible idea. It was not in her nature to diminish herself. Not for anyone.

Some men wanted a woman that would play small. A woman who wouldn't let herself shine. Mimi was not such a woman. For her to settle down, she needed to find a man who could celebrate her. And her wins. Just like Boudicca had found a man who appreciated her strengths, and just as Joan had found a man who called out her true self, so Mimi needed a man who was…man enough…for her.

A quick glance over at Sam's tense shoulders and clenched jaw sent a ribbon of…something through her. Pity? Empathy? Curiosity? She couldn't define it. He was vexing, if nothing else. Older than her by a decade, he was mature in ways she couldn't even imagine. It didn't stop her from trying…but she had no sense of the experiences he had. And if she were being honest with herself, she meant experiences with women. Not that she wanted to know his precise, personal experiences with women…but he was so much older than her, she couldn't help wondering what he could teach her in the bedroom. Again…not him, specifically, but a man his age. Someone like him, but not him.

He was too arrogant by half, and she knew how he felt about her.

She continued her study and noticed that he was in a huff. He roughly dropped the arrows on a nearby barrel and he was about to take off.

Hmm…that didn't sit right with her. She didn't want him to leave. At least, not in the mood that he was in. She didn't like him. Him and his arrogant, condescending demeanor, but she also didn't wish evil upon him. Even if he had basically called her a child. Well, that was a reason to let the man storm off. But…

It wasn't reason enough.

And as always, words that should have been filtered poured effortlessly out of her mouth.

"Arm wrestle me," she blurted out.

"What?" Of course that was what he said. Really, there was no other response—appropriate or otherwise—to a woman demanding an arm wrestle from a man.

"Mimi," Nobi rebuked sharply but mostly in disbelief. Why, an arm wrestle of all things, caused such disbelief, Mimi couldn't pinpoint. She had done countless incredulous activities over the years. Apparently this was one of them.

"Nobi," Mimi sighed. "Do you really think those chastisements are effective?"

A blush crept up her sister's neck. In another situation, Mimi might have checked in with her sister about her comment, but in this moment, she was more concerned about Sam. For some odd reason.

Repositioning herself to catch his eye, she repeated her suggestion, "The next activity should be an arm wrestle."

"That's ridiculous." He turned his profile to her giving Chris and Nobi a look as if to call for some kind of support.

Both parties shrugged in reply.

"Why is it ridiculous?" she prodded.

And then he spoke in a way she had never heard before. He growled at her, "Because I'm a grown man and you're a child. It's not a competition."

"I'm not a child. I'm a mature woman. I can hold my own." Her hands were on her hips and steam was pouring out her nostrils. Or something like it.

She shouldn't have to say those words aloud. It was obvious that she was a woman. He should be able to see it. The man just needed to take a look at her ample bosom to recognize her womanly status, but he had never done that. Not that she wanted him to see that or look at her that way, but really, she had been of age for a while. Had debuted years ago. To some, she was close to being on the shelf. But apparently, in his eyes, she was just the youngest sister.

He took a step closer to her and she could see the potency of the dare in his eyes. Little did he know that she never backed down from a dare, verbalized or implied.

"I'll annihilate you," he said with aplomb.

She faked a laugh. "So be it." They stood toe to toe in the most unprecedented stance. She a ball of fire, him a ball of fury. Her hands on her hips. His across his chest. Both blowing out large, loud puffs of air from their nostrils.

"And don't you dare let me win," she announced after realizing how long the beat of silence lasted.

"I. Would. Never."

When she turned on her heel, she purposely let her elbow knock into his crossed arms. He probably didn't even flinch, but she was a woman possessed. Nothing was going to stop her. From doing what? She wasn't sure yet. But she was on a mission.

"Nobi!"

"Chris!"

One shouted after the other, beckoning their respective parties to join them.

"We need witnesses," she justified.

"I couldn't agree more." How he was speaking with his teeth clenched together so tightly was beyond impressive.

Reluctantly, Chris stood to the side of the barrel while Nobi cleared its surface of the arrows. Mimi dug her elbow into the wood at the same time as Sam.

"I don't understand what we're doing," Chris mumbled.

"It's obvious there is nothing we can do to stop them," Nobi murmured back. "At this point I think we're just here to ensure they don't kill each other."

"I can hear you, Nobi." Mimi blew the hair off her forehead. "No one's going to kill anyone." She was speaking to Nobi, but her eyes were catapulting rocks at Sam. When he said nothing, she raised her eyebrows in a silent question.

"Agreed. No murder. Today."

"Good. Let's proceed." She wiggled her fingers, anticipating his grasp. His fingers folded around hers.

What she hadn't anticipated was the warmth she would feel from his palm, firmly pressed into hers. A perfect fit. His fingers wrapped around her, unrelenting. He would not let go until he won. And she knew he would win. That was the point in this stupid tirade. Compete in something at which she knew he would win to allow him to feel better about himself. But what wasn't the point was to feel her insides turn gooey. As in straight treacle. She straightened her legs and bent at the hip for a better angle. Her breasts were on display, but she didn't care. Apparently he didn't either. His eyes didn't leave her face.

The force and intensity of his gaze combined with the stronghold he physically had on her body was all consuming.

Something sparked within her.

She wasn't sure if she liked it or not.

But she didn't have time to analyze the moment as Chris placed his hand atop their entwined fingers.

"Are you sure about this?"

"Yes," they both said together.

"I would just like to verbalize my dissent on this activity. Again," Chris said with a sigh.

"Noted," Sam replied.

"If you don't want to do it, Nobi will step in." Mimi said it without acknowledging her sister, since she knew she would do it. She was always there to support her, even in crazy antics such as this.

From her peripheral vision, Mimi saw Chris put his hand up, assumingly to stop Nobi from replacing him. "I've got this, Mimi."

With a final shake of his head, he started the countdown. "Three. Two. One."

When the last sound staggered off his tongue, Mimi pushed with all her might. She was strong. She knew it because she and her sisters were very active. They were always engaged in some physical activity. Fencing, knife-throwing, archery, shooting, and more. Nearly every day, they trained in their Practice Hall back at Bellator Manor. It was a priority to each of them to remain healthy and strong. Mimi had witnessed other women struggle to lift a bag or push a piece of furniture even a short distance. She had always been able to do what they couldn't. So when she pushed—with all her might—against Sam's hand, she expected something to happen. But all she did was push.

Against a wall.

No, a mountain.

A mountain made of pure diamond.

There was no budge. Of course, she knew he would be stronger than her. She would be a fool to think she even had a chance. But as she pushed against his hand of metal, she realized she was *that* fool. There was the tiniest part of her that thought she had a chance. Her eyes met his. There was a strain in them. A tension she couldn't make out.

Was he exerting his full strength against her? She dug deeper within herself and pushed harder. His arm bent back.

Hope danced in her heart. Did she have a chance? Was he in

some state of weakness that she could take advantage of? Did she want to take advantage of him? But was it taking advantage of him if he willingly entered the competition?

Deuced devil of a man. She would be her best. Nothing less.

Looking at her grasp, she pushed against his hand with all her might. Incidentally, a grunt escaped her throat at the same time. A bead of sweat dripped down between her breasts. But it was all worth it because his arm bent back further.

But then…he hummed. She peeked up into his eyes and was met by merriment.

God, blast—

"Well done," was all he said as he slowly inched their hands back to center.

"Very well done," was what he said as he gradually pushed their hands down to her side.

"I'm impressed," was his final statement as he gently tapped her knuckles against the wood.

Her hand went limp in his, but still he held on.

It was his win. She knew it was going to be. It was predicted. Expected. Typical. There was still a twinge of some kind in her mind, and also her heart. Her thoughts were growing cluttered and emotions of all sorts were crowding her.

In a rare moment of self-control, she simply said, "You won."

"Yes, I did." Still holding her hand, he asked, "Did you think it would be otherwise?"

She gave him a half shrug. That was noncommittal enough of an answer. But she couldn't leave it at that. "There. I beat you when you weren't your best, and you beat me at something I'm not best at. We're even."

Eyes and hands locked, he said, "That's ridiculous."

"Is it?"

He huffed. "It is."

"Fine. We'll have to settle this over a different challenge at a later time."

"What kind of challenge?" he eyed her warily.

And that question sparked some interest in her. There were a plethora of options for how they could compete.

"You have stars in your eyes," he observed in a monotone voice.

And as monotone as his tone was, hers was inversely enthused. Excitement bubbled over at the possibilities for how the two of them could compete. "I do!"

"How would you be able to confirm that fact?"

"I can feel it." And she could feel her eyes beaming.

"I'm concerned."

"You needn't be." She wasn't sure the reassuring statement held the assurance he was looking for, so she ensured to expand. "We'll find a competition that we both agree upon. No one shall have the upper hand." She continued despite his raised brows. "Perhaps it shall be a bet of some kind."

"I'll win," he interjected.

"You can't possibly know that."

"I can. I don't take bets I won't win." The way he was suppressing his emotions was irritating. Wasn't he excited at the prospect of more competitions?

"That's no fun. Where's the risk in that? The uncertainty? The adventure? The thrill of the unknown?"

"I find that elsewhere," he answered calmly.

"Well, we shall simply find a different activity. Horseback riding—"

"I'd beat you in that, too."

"God, you're insufferable. I don't even want to ask how you can say that."

"I choose the best horses."

"I didn't ask."

"Yet I supplied. I'm a very generous man."

Ugh. This man. There was no winning with him. Well, not on this ridiculous topic. Her stomach growled. Of course…it was the perfect time. Perhaps her body was intervening where her mind wouldn't let go of the silly competition about finding a competition for the two of them to compete in.

"Was that—"

She didn't let him finish. He just would be the type to address something so personal and what some might consider embarrassing. Well, she wouldn't give him the satisfaction of even trying to humiliate her. She would speak for herself.

"This matter is to be discussed at a later time. I'm hungry now."

"Fine."

"I need my hand back."

With a small startled look, he released her hand with the same speed he had let go of the bow earlier when taking his shots.

It had been a morning full of releasing. Full of winnings and releases. Yet, something within her was wound very tightly.

CHAPTER FIVE

H AD HE HONESTLY just arm wrestled a woman? What in the world had made him think that was a good idea? There was no winning against a lady in an arm wrestle. He either won, because, well, really, he was a man and was significantly stronger than her. Or he lost and she would know it was because he let her win. Because, again, his biceps. He shouldn't have to explain it to himself, yet he needed the reminder.

Why, of all the activities that she could have picked, had she chosen an arm wrestle? And why couldn't he just say no? In the moment, it had felt ridiculous, but something about her was hard to resist. Not in any one particular way…just in general. There was something about her that caused him to react, and apparently that included agreeing to arm wrestles.

Maybe he was too irked from losing against her in archery. His mind was a mess. But he had done what he needed to in order to put rest to the worries about his cousin. His most important possessions were locked up safely at Chris's estate. No one knew about that, and even if they did, no one knew what he had or where he was stashing it. So, even though having his maleficent cousin at his own house was unnerving, it wasn't really worrisome. And it wouldn't be until he returned home. At most, it should feel like a problem for another day. He was even hoping that by the time he returned home, his cousin would have left. Of course, that was probably too hopeful.

For all intents and purposes, he should not have such a scrambled mind. But even though Sam wanted to blame his loss and subsequent poor decision-making on external factors, it was a weak connection at best.

Perhaps his mind was just scrambled because of Mimi. All of their encounters were laden with conflict. They rubbed each other the wrong way. He went up, and she went down. Uh…that was a weird way of saying it. Regardless, they were like oil and water. They were too competitive with themselves and others to be of any good to each other. She was loud and independent, and he was…well, he was just selfish. He didn't want to be with anyone, so why the hell was he putting so much thought into it? She pulled him one way or the other and stretched his patience. So really, because he knew she was at this house party rather unchaperoned, all he needed to do was make sure she didn't do any irreparable damage around him. She was a friend of sorts after all.

Now, the question was…who would she be more likely to do that irreparable damage to? Herself or others? Because it certainly wouldn't be done to Sam. He was much too conscientious and callous to let a little thing like her affect him in any negative way. She wasn't reckless, so if anything, she would do damage to herself. And based on everything he knew about her so far, that damage would likely be made against her reputation. So yes, he had his work cut out for him since she had no one else to look out for her.

"What the devil was that about?" Chris asked as the two entered the drawing room for tea. It was about time to join the house party and see a few guests, namely their host.

"I have no idea," Sam replied, rubbing his hand. There was no pain in it from the arm wrestling. Arm wrestle? He was still in a state of shock that he had arm wrestled a woman. Well, it was less of an arm wrestle and more of a show. He knew he was going to win. He easily sized up her biceps before the activity had even been suggested.

"Did she think she could beat you?" Chris's face was half writ with concern and curiosity.

"I doubt it."

"Then why did she suggest it?"

"She's an oddity. That's for sure." Oddity. That wasn't even the right word to describe her. She was uniquely her. No apologies. No shame. And often no explanations.

Sam entered the room, immediately taking notice of several guests milling about. Sally, their hostess's daughter, was drinking tea in the middle of a pack of eager single ladies. Yes. There was a caution sign sticking out of the dirt right in front of that section of the room.

Note to Sam, avoid that coterie at all costs. He could hear the honey dripping from the lips as they asked about wedding plans, if the groomsmen were bachelors (which they were supposed to be), and as a side note, what flowers she had decided upon. If he didn't feel obligated as a friend to be at the wedding, he wouldn't be attending. He didn't even plan on attending a wedding of his own, why would he want to attend someone else's?

Sam's eyes continued their prowl of the room and landed on the Duke of Vanic. "It's been a while since we've seen Roger." There was a man who was another oddity of sorts, but in a completely different way. How did one describe Roger? Usually one would start with a person's unique attributes...well, that was part of the problem. Roger was the epitome of average or commonplace. Conversation with him could be stilted...or boring at best. But anything beat wedding talk.

"Let's greet the old boy," Chris agreed, taking steps toward the mantelpiece where Roger was resting his hand.

"Vanic, where does a man find a good drink in here?"

Roger nodded to the footman who had just entered the room carrying a tray. "Thank God, not everyone is here for tea."

Chris snagged two glasses and shared one with Sam.

Ah, yes...and there was the silence. The awkwardness. Roger sipped his drink looking at nothing in particular. Probably thinking of nothing in particular. And for those reasons, Sam had nothing in particular he wanted to say to the man.

Alas, his options were limited. Roger had always been the man that was invited for the indiscreet purpose of making up numbers, and of course, he was a duke, so that always helped. The man was amiable enough…but was being amiable enough really what a person strove for in life? The man walked around like the color beige. Noticeable only if one was looking for beige, otherwise he blended into his surroundings.

And then he remembered one thing about Vanic that was mildly interesting.

"How's your hand been at archery? Any tournaments of late?"

The small twitch of Roger's eyebrow indicated his attention had shifted to Sam. From what…he wasn't sure.

"I'm always practicing. No tournaments recently. But hopefully soon."

That was a little bit more than Sam expected, but much less than a man would hope for in a conversation.

"What kind of bow do you use?"

"Same as always."

Yes…there was the enthralling conversation, free flowing…Just when Sam thought he would have to think of more to ask, Roger supplied more information.

"Bought an incredible quiver the other day. Last of its kind. I'm hoping to break it in soon." His eyes almost shone as he spoke about his purchase.

But then no questions were asked to either Sam or Chris. This was definitely a one-sided effort.

Sam took another sip of his drink letting Chris pick up the riveting dialogue. The slight burn tickled its way down his throat, and a prickling sensation crept up the back of his neck. He let his eyes roam the room again and caught sight of Mimi. She was staring at him. Curious, that.

He had never caught her gaze on him like this before. He

shifted on his feet and transferred his glass to his other hand. Wanting to look away but not out of discomfort, he held her stare for a second longer. Then another. When her eyes didn't flicker, he realized the truth. She wasn't staring at him, she was studying Roger.

Roger, Duke of Vanic, had captured her attention. The most wild, opinionated woman that he knew was ogling the most boring, underwhelming man of his acquaintance.

Well…

Hmm…

Sam took another sip to make it appear as though everything was normal and that he wasn't trying to swallow the odd-shaped reality he could see forming before his very eyes and then feel forming in his throat. He nearly choked on the small sip he took.

Chris patted him hard on the back. A splutter. A cough.

And then an actual eye from Mimi rested upon him. Except it wasn't the same curious—one might even say dreamy—eye that had befallen Vanic.

No, Sam was not the recipient of such an eye. He received the raised-to-the-roof brow, questioning his most basic competencies. Drinking.

Losing in archery to a woman who closed both of her eyes. Beating said woman in an arm wrestle. Choking on his drink in front of said woman. This was not his morning. Surely, the house party could not get any worse. It was only up from here on out.

"Do you think it's going to rain this week?" That was the brilliant question Chris was asking Roger while Sam collected his bearings.

He was not one to be easily rattled. So what if the morning wasn't going as he had planned. It was not important. All that mattered was how he reacted to it and chose to move forward.

Not willing to take another sip quite yet, Sam exchanged hands with the drink again. He took a quick glance up at Mimi, discreetly, but she was back to observing Roger. And this time, Sam allowed himself to take a longer look at her, and he could see that she was plotting. He didn't know how, but he could just tell that her mind was concocting some grand scheme, and it involved Roger.

Sam slapped Roger on the back, jostling him out of the rain conversation. "God, I hope you're ready for this house party."

Roger and Chris gave Sam a dubious look. The kind of look a person gave a man when they completely understood the words he was saying but not the meaning or the timing of them. He may as well have said that there was a rooster in the room strutting about. Yes, a cock trying to prove himself. But whose?

Well, someone was strutting. It was Mimi. She was headed straight toward them, Nobi in tow with slightly widened eyes.

Mimi's eyes on the other hand looked dreamy, or was that cloudy? Upon closer inspection, Sam couldn't be sure.

Regardless, it looked as though a storm of some kind was brewing, and rain was surely in the forecast. In hindsight, that weather conversation was quite apropos.

Mimi opened her mouth to speak forming the shape of an *O*, when Chris jumped in. "It's going to be such a lovely wedding, isn't it?" Not exactly the most manliest of conversation topics, but Sam didn't want to be a picky beggar at this point.

"Indeed," Nobi replied.

"And how proud are you that Joan and James played such an integral role in uniting the bride and groom?" Chris asked to further the conversation.

Nobi nodded her agreement. Mimi piped up, "We all played a role in it."

"Oh?" Sam challenged her with one word, and he could see the defiance rise up within her like a squall.

"Yes. We did. Isn't that right, Nobi?" She nudged her sister but didn't wait for any form of affirmation before plowing on. "Someone needed to spread the gossip about Jacob's...status..to pique Sally's interest."

"So you were the origin of all the salacious tidbits?" Sam asked.

Mimi's cheeks turned red but she obviously ignored the embarrassment, for she continued to trod forward. "Not all of them, actually," she narrowed her gaze at him, "just the good pieces."

He could have sworn he saw her wink to punctuate her last sentence, but really, he had to doubt that. Didn't he?

While Sam stood stupefied—though hopefully not obviously—Chris filled in. "We're just happy to see a happy couple." An elbow bumped into his kidney. "Aren't we?"

"So happy," Sam mumbled. "Delighted."

Roger had been silent, as per his usual, for the entire conversation, so Sam appreciated when he finally did speak. "Well, it stands to reason that with happy people we shall have a diverting house party," Roger summarized. "Excuse me." And with that, he quit the group in search of another drink. Or another conversation. It didn't matter.

Roger was not an easily stimulated or amused fellow, so the fact that he thought something was going to be amusing was terrifying to Sam. Most assuredly, terrifying. A shiver ran down his back.

"Mimi, shall we take some tea?" Nobi spoke the words as a suggestion, but they sounded like a plea.

"I think that's a...*delightful* idea." Oh. The chit was mocking him. He shouldn't be surprised. She wasn't the type to hold back, and she had certainly mocked him before. But the way she said *delightful*...he couldn't erase the tone from his ears, and for a split second he wondered what she might truly find delightful.

"If that's what you want, you should do it." Perhaps it was an odd thing to say, but in the moment, Sam knew that nothing could convince him to sit at the table and drink tea talking about weddings, flowers, and love.

"You'll see soon enough, Duke," Mimi leaned in to say. "I always get what I want."

Yes. That was the appropriate word for what was about to manifest. Terrifying.

CHAPTER SIX

IF TEA WAS terrifying, dinner was disastrous. It was one thing for Mimi to approach them and not so subtly vie for Roger's attention; it was an entirely separate matter for her to waltz into dinner wearing that.

That.

Her dress was a crimson red pulling out the color of her lips, contrasting with the sky in her eyes. Her blonde tresses were loosely tucked at the back of her head looking as though they could fall free at any moment. The analogy was not lost on Sam. And...Sam almost spluttered when he saw them, her breasts...they were on display. He had to convince himself that what he was seeing was in fact not her areola.

But those mounds...those creamy white mounds...of a woman. This was not a child. This was a woman on a mission. Golden earrings framed her face and a small chain rested snuggly just above her decolletage. But that was the nice word for what Sam was witnessing.

Exactly as he had predicted, this woman was on a path to destruction. Her reputation was hanging in the balance. It would either go one way or the other. Society would accept this decision (this dress) as an anomaly, or they would crucify her. She had the eccentricity that might just lend well to the option of this night being an anomaly. She also had a brother-in-law who was a duke (thanks to Boudicca) and an impending duke for her second brother-in-law (thanks to Joan). It was unusual indeed for sisters to all claim a duke, but Sam pushed that thought aside. Well, more accurately, that thought was pushed aside by Mimi's flouncing breasts.

They were bouncing so lightly against the ridge of fabric that he was sure one of them was about to pop out and introduce herself.

Wouldn't that be something? How would he respond? Shock would surely be his one and only response.

Then again…there was always a good handshake in response to an introduction. After all, he was a man, and those creamy mounds looked delectable. Not because they were hers…but just because, well, breasts. They were meant to be licked, nipped, sucked. His hands would itch to massage them, squeeze them gently to see her reaction—not *her* reaction, per se.

This was not going well. That dress needed to go. Then she'd be left dressless. Wait. The dress had to stay. She just needed to cover up—dammit.

"Your Grace," Mimi drawled from Sam's side, and despite the tone of her voice entwining itself with his breath, momentarily causing a lapse in what should have been an average inhalation, she was in fact not addressing him but Roger. With little heed paid to ceremonious seating arrangements, Mimi had been placed between Roger and Sam, while Chris and Nobi had been seated further away. Joan and James were so far down the table that they could hardly be seen, but they were probably enjoying that. They likely had plans to slip away at some point.

"Isn't this a lovely house party?" Mimi's unusually vapid question targeted Roger.

"Indeed," came the curt reply. Vanic was no more interested in her questions than the extraneous utensils bordering his plate. And that was still less interest than he had paid the woman's wardrobe, or, all out call for attention. That is to say, the man observed, appreciated, nothing.

Mimi reached for her glass and somehow managed to bump

Roger's arm in the process. "Apologies," she whispered.

The man didn't even look at her, just mumbled. "Not to worry."

A fake trill of a giggle, like none that Sam had witnessed before (and prayed fervently he would never have to be present for again) escaped Mimi's lips.

Sam couldn't help himself. He cleared his throat and called for Mimi's attention. "What are you doing exactly?" he hissed.

She kicked him under the table in reply.

"Ow! What was that for?"

Her head whipped around like a snake sensing its prey, but instead of a slithering tongue, she barely opened her mouth to grit out, "I'm having a conversation." And then, because he assumed she couldn't help herself, she added, "Unlike *some* people."

"A conversation?" He eyed her body up and down. "Is that what you call this?"

A quick nod and she turned her attention back to Roger. Otherwise known as The Wall. The Bland White Wall Lacking Typical Ducal Discourse. TBBWWLTDD for short. Sam snickered to himself.

"I do hope there will be some archery activities at this house party, don't you?" Mimi pitched another question at Vanic.

Roger gave her a brief side eye and continued eating. "That would be nice." Another spellbinding rejoinder from Roger.

"I do love the feel of a bow in my hand."

Silence.

"To hit the target with such accuracy always gives me a sense of pride. Wouldn't you agree?"

"If I must."

Sam choked back a laugh covering it with a cough. He was certain—well, he was almost certain—that Roger hadn't meant that to be rude.

But this was torturous to watch. The woman had no idea what she was doing. Was she flirting? This could not be her idea of attracting a man's attention, could it? Her attire screamed wanton and her conversation topics vacillated between conveying her as a bore and a hoyden. Which was it? She needed to present one image to Roger. Herself.

Sam groaned. Apparently aloud. He only knew this because the moment the groan left his mouth, Mimi whipped her head around again and whispered, "Do you mind? Some of us are enjoying a pleasant dinner conversation."

"Some? You mean you?" The words were out before he could analyze them properly.

Her eyebrows went up while her eyelids went down. With a slight lift of her chin, her eyes fluttered back open and she said, "Not just me."

If this were Sam attempting to capture a woman's attention and he was doing what Mimi was doing, he would want someone to say something. Quickly. To appear incompetent was not an option. And Mimi…well, she was the epitome of an incompetent flirt. But did she know it? Was she in denial? Or was she aware of it and proceeding onward valiantly anyway? Was she brave or oblivious?

Ugh.

"Sam, please." A whispered admonishment along with a kick.

Oh. She wasn't getting away with it this time. Once her foot landed on the ground, he placed his booted toe on hers.

A muffled grunt expelled from Mimi's throat. "Stop that," she said while trying to wiggle her slippered toe free.

"I don't think so. I can no longer be witness to what you call flirting." Ah. This was much better. Mimi was struggling with her recent detainment, and he could eat his peas in peace.

He was pretty sure he had a smug look on his face, mostly because Mimi said, "Wipe that smug look off of your face."

He did no such thing.

But when Mimi turned herself to face her plate head on, he could feel an energy emitted from her body. And he sensed that her attentions had shifted. It was a good thing. He wouldn't have to witness her cringeworthy attempts at seduction.

Until he felt her misplaced attention on his ankle. Mimi had slipped her toes free from their slipper and was slowly trailing them up his shin. He felt a slight twitch in his cock. But he kept his foot firmly in place over hers.

What the—

"Are you enjoying the meat?"

"Ahem. What…" and he meant to finish that question. Really, he did. Only her toes were trailing up and down his calf. With pressure. A light massage to the backs of his legs. And he almost unwittingly freed her foot, but some sliver of resolve kept his boot in place while she massaged his leg muscle with her toe.

He blinked. Surely it wasn't a longer than average blink.

And then her hand was on his knee. Daintily. Like a tickle. A tickle that almost made him laugh, or smirk at the least. But he held himself together. But the chit wasn't done yet. Her hand was drifting up his thigh—

He pushed himself closer to the table and grabbed her hand with his. Her silky soft hand rested in his. Earlier he had arm wrestled this dainty hand when she had been using all her strength against him, but this soft, smooth skin against his was now a weapon of a different kind.

"Stop it." He glared at her, daring her to make her next move. No, not daring her. That was the last thing he wanted to do. If he dared her…how far would she go? Inwardly he shook his head. He didn't want to know the answer to that question. But he did.

"Stop acting…like that."

She batted her eyelashes mockingly. "Like what?"

"Like a—"

"Ah, ah, ah. Be careful, Sam. It's just"—her eyes darkened in fierce competition—"an innocent little battle of the wills. Wouldn't you agree?"

Batte? Yes. Wills? Hell, yes. Innocent? Far from it. But the chit wasn't letting up, and he needed to do something. Quickly.

He changed his tactic. "Please." It was hardly spoken above a whisper, but he saw the second she registered the cautionary plea in his voice. He wasn't begging. He wasn't making himself vulnerable. He was making himself proper and asking her to do the same. Put aside the competition. Whatever it was they were competing for, and be respectful. Would she acquiesce? He could only hope.

Her brows knitted together and she flew a seething glare at him. Then she extracted her hand from his thigh and her toe from his calf, leaving a line of heat flowing between the two places.

She spent the rest of dinner making the most asinine comments to Roger who answered her with the bare minimum that etiquette required. He didn't think he would appreciate her attention redirected at Roger, but it was better this way. For now, at least.

Couldn't she see the disinterest? Why the devil was she trying so hard? She must know that she could have any man in the room. Well, not any man. Not him. Sam wasn't the marrying type. But any other single man was available for her taking.

The chit needed his help.

And he wanted to help her. If only so he never had to witness such an agonizing interaction again.

"I try to practice every day," Mimi was still talking.

Finally, Roger looked at her. Not exactly with any admiration, in fact, one would say it was with the opposite of admiration, if bemused curiosity was its opposite.

"You?"

And then Sam realized that Roger hadn't really been listening at all.

"You consider yourself an archer?" Roger asked. Sam couldn't interpret if the question was asked with incredulity or derision. But whatever laced his tone caused Mimi to sit a little straighter.

He hoped it was her defensive posture. Or aggressive. That would work just as well. A woman ought to stand up for herself.

But when she spoke, her tone was cheery. As if she were happy to have received even that pathetic amount of attention.

"Yes, as a matter of fact, I do consider myself an archer. Quite a good one. In fact earlier today, with no—"

"Roger," Sam interrupted out of desperation, realizing where Mimi was taking the conversation. Yes, a woman ought to stand up for himself, but not at the cost of his dignity. "We shall play a game of piquet later this evening." It was rude to interrupt. It was more rude to speak over Mimi to a guest that wasn't to Sam's immediate left or right, but he didn't care. A change of topic was of the essence. Thank God Roger noticed nothing (again) and eased into a new conversation.

One might think Sam acted out of desperation for his pride. And yes, his dignity was on the line a little bit. (A lot). But even more urgent than this pride was an instinct to protect. That might be putting it too strongly. It was more of an instinct to help. Roger was not the type of man to be interested in a competitive woman. He liked his women passive. If Mimi wanted Roger— which for some asinine reason she did—then Sam would have to consider helping her. That, or be witness to her pitiful attempts at seduction. He could help her get the man she wanted.

Yes. Help. But only if she asked would he help. He wouldn't just go about offering advice to someone who wouldn't appreciate it.

He could help. It was instinctual. The exact opposite of his father. And so long as he never married, he would keep his own healthy instincts intact forever.

CHAPTER SEVEN

Well, THAT WAS a success of sorts. After dinner, Mimi was in the drawing room with Nobi while the men had port together. This period of time in the evening could either be an awkward time, when women engaged in contemplations or worse, small talk, until the men reappeared. Or it could be rich with gossip. This particular evening fell somewhere in between, and she was only too glad to have Nobi around to share conversation.

It was still so fresh to her that she didn't have Boudicca and Joan around. Boudicca being away, and Joan...well, Joan had found a way to always be sneaking off with James during this house party. Soon enough, they would be knee deep in honeymoon season, but for now they were enjoying some stolen moments.

Was it weird that Mimi imagined where the two might sneak off? She didn't care. If it were her, she would want to find a closet or a wardrobe somewhere. Just the idea of being in an enclosed space with limited room to move made her feel a little faint. She could just imagine the crushing of bodies and the urgency she would feel being taken by a tall dark-haired man with a strong jaw... or whomever she was being taken by.

Yes. The wardrobe sounded delicious. Though...come to think of it...out on the grass atop a hill with the chance of being caught...oooh...that sent a thrill up her spine. Not for her first time, but she could envision herself agreeing (easily) to be laid down on a swatch of plush grass with a heavy body heating her from above. She could almost feel the light prickles from the blade of grass poking her arms. The sky above. Vast. Open. Anything was allowed. Yet the forbiddenness of it, the chance of being caught, that was the additional spark she knew could heat her up. She pictured herself on the hill as a man came into view lying over her. Dark hair, rich brown eyes, thick biceps, yet with a condescending look. It seemed out of place considering Roger had light hair. She couldn't shake it. The face belonged to someone she knew. Whose face was that that came to her mind—

"Mimi, please tell me what possessed you to wear that dress this evening." Nobi reached out and brushed a lock of hair behind her ear. "And your hair…what's come over you?"

"It's fate, Nobi," she said, clasping her hands together against her bosom. Perhaps she was showing more than she ought, but that wasn't her main concern right now. Right now, she wanted to relish in her relative success. Roger looked at her. Spoke to her. Some words at least. And she was pretty sure she had caught his interest over archery. Now she needed to make a plan for how to connect with him over the activity. Her eyes closed as she began to dream of an archery tournament in which she would go head-to-head with Roger. Who knows who would win…likely her. And when she did, Roger would sweep her up into his arms and carry her off to his—

"Mimi." Nobi nudged her arm. "Open your eyes. You look ridiculous."

Without even opening her eyes, Mimi knew her sister was upset with her. It took more than a little annoyance for Nobi to be anything but polite. So she flung her eyelids up and lifted her chin to her sister's visage.

"I don't think I look ridiculous, and neither does Roger."

A deep furrowing of Nobi's brow indicated her concern, but Mimi knew she had nothing to worry about. So why the look of…oh, was that pity?

Nobi placed a gentle hand on her forearm, "Darling, he didn't even notice you."

Well, that was just patently untrue. Her hands transferred from the clasp over her heart to the crossing of arms over her chest. "He did, too." There. That should show her.

"Mimi, did the man say more than two words to you?"

"He certainly did. In fact, he said more than three."

Nobi covered a cough, but the pity didn't leave her eyes. Yes, that was a pity. Mimi could see it clearly now, and she most definitely did not like it. Before she could give it much thought, Chris and Sam entered the room having finished their drinks with the men and headed straight to them.

Sam glared at her the entire march across the room, and when he finally arrived in front of her, he tossed her his profile. Chris feigned ignorance to his friend.

"How was your dinner?" he asked in a polite attempt at conversation.

"The same as yours," Mimi bit back. She was not in the mood for the shallowness of etiquette.

Sam scoffed, but said nothing.

"You have something to say, Sam?" she drawled his name finally securing his gaze.

"Everything I have to say I already said to you."

"Your scoff says otherwise. Why don't you just say what's on your mind? I'm a big girl, I can—"

"That's just it. You're a girl in woman's clothing—"

"I'm a woman of marrying age looking for a husband." The hem of her dress covered the toes of his shoes, her chest was heaving in front of him. The man infuriated her. "You have no idea what you're talking about."

"I know more than you."

"No, you don't."

"Yes, I do."

"No, you don't."

"Yes. I. Do."

"Prove it," Chris interjected the budding insanity.

"What?" Sam and Mimi both asked at the same time.

"I said, prove it, Sam. If you know so much, advise the young girl—woman." He gave Mimi an apologetic look which she dismissed, because really, that slip of the tongue was the least of her concerns.

"I wouldn't take advice from him if he were the last man on earth." Mimi turned her shoulder to be perpendicular to his chest.

"That suits me just fine, since I wouldn't give her advice if she was the last woman in the *galaxy*."

Ooooh. Just to show her up, he had to emphasize *galaxy* over earth. That dratted man!

"I'd rather take advice from Chris." The second the words were out of her mouth, she knew they were the wrong thing to say. Everyone in the group knew why, too, but she didn't want to bring attention to it anymore than she had already.

Chris broke the silence.

"That's settled then. Each of you knows more than the other, but neither is willing to rise to the challenge and prove it," Nobi added quietly with an altogether too smug of a smile. "Shall we carry on with the rest of the evening?" She held her hand out for Chris to take. "I feel like a nice game of whist."

"Let's." Chris took her hand and the two turned and made their way to a table set up with cards.

Thus leaving Sam glaring at Mimi and Mimi shooting daggers at Sam.

Sam was too old for her. Ahem—for her to listen to. The man smelled of tea and whiskey. Old man scents that did absolutely nothing to stimulate the inner workings between her legs. He would know nothing about how she could go about seducing a man. He would understand nothing about her. Probably tell her that she had to change herself for a man to be attracted to her. Well, if she wanted to change herself she would do it in her own damn time. In her own way. Hadn't she changed how she dressed to attract Roger?

Yes, she could change some things if she wanted to. That was the key, if she wanted to. No one was going to convince her to do something she didn't want to do. And if she wanted to flaunt herself, dangle herself, throw herself prostrate in front of Roger, she damn well would. If…she wanted to.

The only way to shut Sam up had been to beat him. When he had clamped down on her foot at dinner, she absolutely had to respond. Her body ached to respond to him. Beat him. Show him who she was. What she was made of. So…she slid her toe up his strong, muscly leg. The effect had been immediate. His body had stiffened, and she could see his molars clenching a farthing between them. Now…it was true that those muscles had called to her toes and her toes had taken a slight detour from her original plan. But massaging the back of his calf had been key to keeping him distracted.

The hand on his thigh though…that was genius. She half grinned recalling it. Again, not part of any calculated plan she had, but it somehow all worked perfectly for her good.

"What are you smirking about?" he gritted out.

"Wouldn't you like to know?"

"Not sure why I asked," he mumbled, looking around the room. "I need a drink."

"I suppose you really think you could play God in this situation, don't you?"

Another scoff. This time followed by an explanation. "If I wanted to play God and match you with Roger, I *know* I could. There is no doubt in my mind I could help you secure him as a husband." A drink tray passed by and he grabbed a glass. Taking a sip, she watched him drain the fluid. And for some inexplicable reason, she clenched her thighs together while she studied the liquid pouring down his throat.

"But not only wouldn't I advise you if you were the last—"

"Yes, yes. We all heard."

He chuckled. "Well, I also wouldn't advise you because he's

completely wrong for you."

Wrong for her? Bah! Of all the nerve. The man really did have no clue what he was talking about. And her only response was a giggle.

"You find that funny?"

"You're already playing God, thinking you know best."

"Perhaps. But the man isn't interested in you."

"Of all the nerve—"

"Oh." With a slightly shocked look in his eye, he stared at her. "You don't know..." A flash of pity crossed his face and then something else took over.

"I don't need your pity." She tossed a few loose strands of hair behind her head. "You have your opinion and I have mine."

"Your opinion is wrong if you think Roger is interested in you."

Blasted man. Couldn't he just drop the conversation? He had no right telling her how to live her life. Discouraging her. Deterring her from her destiny. But she wasn't going to say that. She wasn't going to encourage his solicitedness. He could keep his advice to himself. She didn't need it. Didn't want it. She knew her destiny. Fate had spoken to her. When Roger and she had reached for the same quiver, she knew—with absolute certainty—that he was part of her destiny. And she would keep that secret to herself. She was the only one who appreciated its depth anyway. It was a secret she could share with Nobi, but otherwise she would take it to her grave. There was no way on earth she would share that piece of information with Sam. Not if he was the last man on—in the galaxy!

"It's fate." It slipped out. She couldn't have stopped it if she had clamped her hand over her mouth. She still would have said it.

"Pardon me?"

She shrugged her shoulders carelessly. Fine. She had said it, but she didn't need to say it again. If he heard, he heard, and if he hadn't—

"Fate?"

Damn him.

"Yes." Well, there was no turning back now. "It's fate. Roger and I are meant to be together."

Sam cleared his throat. "And what, pray tell, has led you to believe that your destinies are entwined?"

And she could have kept her silence. That would have been for the better. There was no point in explaining something so profound to someone who hardly understood the basics of life and love.

"A quiver."

He choked. A few sputters and a cough followed. People were staring. She patted him none too gently between the shoulders, but he backed away. "I'm fine," he glared at her.

"You didn't seem fine."

He took another sip while staring her dead in the eye, proving his competencies, as if to say, *see?*

"I need more of an explanation than a single word." He returned to the conversation at hand about fate.

"It was two words," she volleyed back.

"Quiver?"

"A quiver."

He rolled his eyes. "Is this about being right or about getting to the truth?"

"Isn't that the same thing?" she winked.

"You're showing your age, Mimi. That's one way to deter Roger."

"Don't all men prefer a younger woman?"

"Younger? Perhaps. Immature? I think not."

She wanted to growl at him.

"Calm yourself," he said while eyeing the room again. It was as though he couldn't deign to look upon her when she didn't act the way he wanted her to. "Don't make a spectacle by growling at me in public."

"Me make a spectacle? Heaven forbid." Her voice was increasing in volume.

"I have no qualms walking away from you if you're going to be immature."

"Me?" her voice squeaked. And even though she knew she was being immature, her body had a mind of its own around him. "I'll be as immature as I want. You don't get to control my actions." Her palms were sweaty and her heart was beating rapidly. At dinner he was indicating to her that she was acting too mature for her age. Now he was telling her that she was behaving too immaturely. Who the deuce was he to police her behavior? And then she recalled his reactions to her "mature" ways.

So, rethinking her tactics, she pushed her chest out slightly, delighted to see his eyes drop for even a split second. When his eyes traced back up over her lips, she said, "And I'll be as mature as I want, whenever I deem it convenient."

"Convenient?" he asked over what sounded like a notch in his throat.

But she didn't answer him. She winked and walked away. It was the perfect time to get an update from Nobi on her game of whist. Forget Sam and his old beckoning bones.

CHAPTER EIGHT

S AM WAS CONVINCED that he would not help Mimi secure Roger's attention if she were the last woman in the galaxy. He had said what he meant and meant what he said. He wouldn't help her if she begged for it. What kind of woman left her fate up to fate? A jangle of rocks was rolling around in Sam's belly just thinking about what utter nonsense that was.

It was obvious to anyone with eyes or ears that Roger was not the least bit interested in Mimi. And if after last night's reckless display there was not even the tiniest fraction of a smile or a gaze or more than a few words shared, surely it was clear that there really was no interest to be had. No matter what Mimi did, there was no hope. If Roger wasn't interested in her brazen opinions, overly competitive nature, and no holds barred approach to life—never mind her shimmering gold locks, suffocatingly vanilla scent, and sky-blue eyes—there was simply no hope of him conjuring it up from nowhere.

But then a pang seared through his heart. He dreaded having to watch Mimi attempt another awkward flirtation. It was like watching a fish out of water. Or watching a cat try to take a bath. No one wanted to be privy to those events. He tried not to think about what the next encounter might be, but he couldn't help himself. Would she do something completely audacious and ask the man to dance? That would give the ladies something to gossip about. Of course it would depend on how she went about it.

Would she simply proffer her hand and expect an invitation? Not likely. This was Mimi. She would be the type to simply ask the question. As if ingrained societal strictures were nothing more than a suggested way of life, and not the living, breathing, executing entity that it was. Still, he could picture her asking Roger to dance.

Or would she try to discreetly ask people about his interests and proclivities? He shuddered at the thought of her attempting a clandestine mission of any kind. She was too…what was the right word to describe someone like her? Someone who always spoke her mind without concern for putting others on the spot. She wasn't inconsiderate…not quite. But she didn't let etiquette dictate her behavior like she ought to. She was a genteel lady after all; she should care about her reputation, especially if she was trying to secure a duke.

He resigned himself to watching her make her own bed and then lie in it. Alone. For no clear reason, a shiver trounced up his spine at the thought.

Dash it. He would have to watch the woman compete for affection and lose. She was a competitor. He had seen it firsthand, and he knew the type. Because he was her type. She needed to rise to the challenge, even if she failed. Nothing was worse than watching a flailing attempt at a win. Being witness to her incompetence in this area—especially after seeing her success so gracefully elsewhere—almost made him want to reconsider. But he would not. Even if she fell flat on her face, he would hold his ground, stand by, and let her fall. It was the best way to learn how to win.

There was no other option. She was too young to take any guidance from an *old man* (her words not his) like him. It rankled that she thought of him as an old man when he was not even a decade her senior. Plenty of men of the *ton* married with a far more disparate age gap. Hell, some seventy-year-old men (balding and toothless) still took a bride in hopes of securing an heir. It was just the way of society. But he could predict how

Mimi would feel about that situation.

A snap of a twig brought Sam to the present. The late morning sun shone through the trees, blinding him momentarily. Chris was a few yards ahead walking with Nobi toward the archery activity. After last night's discussion, Mimi must have convinced Sally to hold an archery tournament of sorts. Despite it being a house party in honor of Sally's engagement, she was more than happy to oblige a dear friend. So many of the house guests were on their way to the same location where a no-eyed Mimi had beaten him in target practice.

Humiliating.

Rather amusing, though. If he allowed himself to chuckle over how flustered he had been. Not one to usually fall prey to the drama of his day, Mimi had really pounced upon him at his lowest. Or close to it.

No. His lowest had been a different day. Far more tragic events. Not something to ponder in the moment.

Now he had to focus on redeeming himself, for he would enter this silly competition. And win. Of course, that.

THUD!

A low moan trembled through the air in front of him where he saw Mimi. Face down in the ground. Well…wonders never cease. Her falling on her face had happened a mite quicker than anticipated.

He sauntered the few steps closer to her and squatted before her. All the others were much further ahead now, leaving them alone.

"You all right?"

"Yes." Her head flew up and she blew a stream up her face to clear her hair from her eyes. Her palms were propped on the ground as she lifted herself just above hovering the ground. He had a straight shot down her dress. To explore the dark valley between her—

"I'm fine," she grunted.

"Are you?" And he wanted to reach out and wipe the dirt off

her cheeks. Of course he didn't do that. He was being ridiculous. The chit was about to learn her lesson, and he needed to step back and allow her to do so. He shot back up, but before he could turn around and let her be, her voice stopped him. Though…not intentionally. She hadn't called out to him. Hadn't reprimanded him for his rudeness. It was just a little mumble. Barely audible in fact.

"I should have expected nothing less."

And he couldn't walk away then. He told his feet to keep moving, but they refused. And he told his mouth to stay shut, but it didn't listen. Really, it had no ears. What could he expect?

"What did you say?" his mouth asked.

"I said," she pushed herself up higher off the ground, and now one foot was beneath her body, "I should have expected nothing less. From you, that is."

"What's that supposed to mean?" The sensation of a snake was slithering up through his organs, warning him that something was about to attack.

"If I have to explain it, there's no point in saying it."

"I rather think that's a terrible way to live life. And more to the point, that's a horrendous approach to arguing. How the bloody hell should I know what you mean when you string obscure words and sentiments together?" That snake was rearing its head, ready to strike.

Mimi glared at him while she appeared to be struggling to get her other foot underneath herself. Sam couldn't determine the issue, but perhaps her foot was caught in the hem of one of her many layers of clothing. She grunted as she lifted her foot but made no progress.

"What's going on with you? Have you got yourself a pair of new shoes?"

"Yes."

Well, that was not expected. But perhaps it should have been.

"I'm borrowing a pair from a friend, if you must know."

He must know. He really must.

"Why? Do you think that a glimpse of the toe of your boot is really going to secure you a husband?"

Her eyebrows raised at him. "Perhaps we could continue the questioning once I'm standing firmly on both feet."

"That might take a while." At his mocking her glare deepened, causing him to slightly rock back on his heels.

"Bah! Help me up, you idiot."

He belted out a laugh. Rarely did anyone other than his closest friends ever talk to Sam in such a way.

If that was her strike, he could easily deflect it. He could just walk away and leave her in the dirt. She needed to learn. How else was she going to become a stronger person? He should just walk away.

But he didn't. She looked so helpless lying there with dirt on her face. Helpless? No. Mimi was anything but helpless. All the same, he crouched down, extended a hand, and opened his mouth.

"I'll offer my help. I'm a gentleman after all. But I'd strongly recommend that you reconsider who the idiot is between us, all things considered."

"I've considered them all and have reached the same conclusion." With a grumble, she took his hand and stood up. None too gently. In fact, she tripped on her hem, and her body stumbled into Sam's.

Her plush body...plied completely against his. Rock hard. Everywhere.

Stunned. He was too stunned to speak. To even think for a split second. This was definitely a woman pressed up against him. A warm-blooded, competitive, competent woman who was about to botch everything up.

It was one thing for Mimi to fail and show weakness in front of him. He didn't mind. After he saw her glory in her win over him in archery, the chit could be brought down a notch. (And arm wrestling him didn't count.)

But what if she metaphorically fell on her face in front of

Roger? Or someone else? Someone who wasn't so accepting of her shortcomings. Someone who might feed the gossip mill. Dinner the other night had been excruciating, but if he was the only witness he wouldn't have been cringing throughout the whole meal.

Something about watching Mimi fail, make a fool of herself, in front of others…no, that didn't sit right with Sam.

She could show him her weaknesses, but others didn't need to be privy to that. It was almost as if that could be a secret between them.

Like the secret he was feeling with her body against his. Her soft curves fit perfectly against his hard contours. He wanted to slip his hand down her bottom, pull her even closer, hold her tightly until there was no space for air to squeeze between them. That was a dangerous thought.

The danger was so sharp it ought to pop the bubble he felt he was still inside.

Holding her latched to his body, it was more than just the weakness that she showed. More than just a vulnerability that she showed. More than just the softness that she showed. It was something in her eyes, like she was seeing through a cloud. Like she was dreaming. Like he was the object of her dreams. The object of her fantasy. But that couldn't be true. He wasn't the type of man single, young, marriage-minded women dreamed about.

A whimper crept out of her lips ripping a hoarse response from his. "What's wrong?"

Was that even his voice? It sounded strained. This was not good.

Her eyes fluttered open. The softest expression he had seen from her. "My pinky."

The look. The tone. The moment. It was a bubble beyond time and space. He heard nothing. Felt nothing. Except the pounding of his heart. Like someone was taking a hammer to it. In an even more gruff voice, he asked, "What's wrong with your pinky?" And since he knew it was wrong for his hand to slip down to her bottom, he covered her hand with his instead.

Was it his imagination or did she suck in a breath at his touch? What universe was he in right now? He couldn't think.

"It…hurts." He had never heard her voice that gentle before. Vulnerable. Open.

"Where?" he asked as he rubbed his fingers along her delicate digit.

"On the knuckle." Her blue eyes gazed up at him through long dark lashes.

"Here? Does this hurt?" He squeezed the place on her finger that she said was sore, and she winced. And her wince gripped his heart.

She nodded while her gaze fell to his mouth. Her tongue darted out and licked her bottom lip.

Her affirmation of pain, even slight, shook him. Everyone felt pain. It was one of the few common threads amongst the human race. He couldn't do much about her pinky, but…the thought that flew through his mind flapped its wings hard. He could prevent her further pain with Roger.

He let the thought float around in his mind, and once the flapping ceased, the thought settled. He could help her. She didn't have to try and win this on her own. There was no additional pride in accomplishing this particular feat on her own. She thought it was fate. Perhaps she already fancied herself in love with Roger. Who was he to question her love? Her choices? He would not stand in the way of love. If pursuing Roger would make her happy, that was what mattered. He wasn't even sure why it mattered so much now, but it did.

The question looming in his head was how to offer her that help. She had been dead set on not accepting any advice from him. Then again, she probably hadn't expected to be standing in his arms for so long either. Perhaps there was a chance it was going to be easier than he expected.

"It feels better now," she whispered, and he couldn't help

watching her lips as she spoke. So engrossed was he by her rose red mouth that he didn't realize he had still been caressing her hand and rubbing her pinky softly between his fingers.

He needed to release her, fingers and all, and go find Chris. A plan had to be put into motion before she could suspect something. He hoped it would work because he liked the idea of making her feel better.

"That's good," he mumbled.

But something inside of him flared up at those two simple words in warning, probably because he realized the first thing he had to do was stand up and get her perfectly fitted body off him.

CHAPTER NINE

MIMI'S BODY WAS trembling as she followed behind Sam toward the targets. She could still feel his body all over hers. Or under, to be more accurate. A shiver, like a string, had been pulled through her, unraveling all her parts. And she was hot. Beyond any heat she had ever known. If merely one section of her body had been seared by him, she could rub that spot in hopes the burn would fade. Alas, no such luck could be had. The entire front of her body was in flames from having collided with him. And not just a brief collision and then parting, no, a full-contact, long exposure melding.

She was extremely grateful to her pinky in this moment. Though the poor thing had suffered, it felt next to no pain now. Yet it had provided her with touches, care, and closeness that she wouldn't be rid of for a long time. Her mind was reeling with the possible outcomes of that scenario. It could lead to so much more touching, and so much more closeness. Her body shivered at the prospect of being pressed to Sam. Well, any man. She was sure that the man could be swapped out and the feelings would remain.

No, the feelings wouldn't remain. That was ridiculous to think. They would be *even better*. So much better because in her fantasies she was always with a man that she couldn't get enough of. A man that she was instantly in love with. Her heart thudded once in front of him and would thud harder forever because of him. That was the makings, the crux of, her fantasies.

Her fantasies had always included a male hero that would sweep her into his arms somehow, but having never been swept, her physical reactions had been left up to herself. And touching herself had never left her feeling even half of the sensations that had just rippled through her.

This was amazing. She couldn't imagine it getting any better, but it must be. If this was the kind of reaction her body had with a man that she didn't even like, imagine what would happen when her body came into contact with Roger. She was sure that she might just explode. And if her body wasn't feeling so heavy and hot from being held by Sam, she would undoubtedly skip onward to the targets. As it was, she needed a moment to calm herself before showing her face to others. Especially Nobi.

Although it was improbable for her body and face to be reflecting the heat she still felt, she was quite sure her face was giving something away. So she had told Sam to go on ahead of her and she would follow shortly.

She willed her body into submission. Telling her heart to stop pounding, knocking on the door of her ribcage as if it were the shackles, rather than the protection from the outside world. And her feet. She commanded those to stop tapping, stop rocking back and forth over to heels and back. Her hands were a trifle more difficult to constrain. The clammy beads of sweat weren't particularly good listeners, and the only action that worked was to swipe them along the fabric of her skirts until the beads learned their lesson; that is, this was not a welcoming time or place for perspiration. Not that she knew any welcoming times or places for a lady to perspire.

Those few extra moments had given her just enough time to commandeer her emotions and school her features to what she hoped was her normal brazen self.

When she joined her sister and Chris, she noticed Nobi fidgeting. Fussing with invisible flint on her sleeve, tucking away already tucked hairs, and shifting her weight slightly from one hip to the other. Birds were chirping in the trees surrounding them, and some of the other guests were sitting on the grass on blankets provided by footmen at the ready. Conversations were flowing. Except between Chris and Nobi.

"What's wrong?"

Chris and Nobi exchanged a glance. Nobi looked away first.

"Nobi?" She watched her sister half shrug one shoulder. "Chris?"

He didn't answer her directly. Instead, he prompted Nobi. "Should I tell her?"

Nobi raised her brows at him as if to say she didn't want Mimi mad at her, so he may as well be the one to break the news.

"Tell me what?" Mimi stamped her foot on the ground. This was getting ridiculous. What would Chris have to tell her that Nobi couldn't do?

Chris cleared his throat, a last attempt at getting approval—or dismissal—from Nobi. "We think you should throw the tournament."

"What?" She couldn't have been more surprised if she had faked it. "Why in the world would I do that?" That was her asking calmly.

"We"—he cleared his throat again, looking one more time for Nobi's encouragement—"think that if you want to sed–secure Roger's attention, that he would respond more favorably if you…didn't beat him."

Oh. He was that type of male, was he? The normal type. The type who couldn't handle a woman besting him.

Well, that was not the type of man Mimi wanted for a husband. Not only that, but she was pretty sure Roger was not actually that type. Otherwise, why would fate lead her to him in such an incontrovertible fashion?

She placed her finger on her cheek. "Let me think about that—no."

"No?" Nobi asked with a half surprised half delighted look. It was the type of indecisive look that admired her response but also questioned it at its core.

"No." Mimi tossed her hair back. "Of course not. I will not throw the tournament. I could no more do that than cut off my own arm."

At that moment, Sam had stepped up and joined the conversation casually, and not as though their bodies had been sandwiched together moments ago. Apparently he wasn't very affected by the event. That made sense. "You would be the kind to cut off your own arm if you needed to."

Well…that was a compliment of sorts. She thought. She supposed if she were desperate, trapped, and her life depended on it, she could do it. She had a strong will to survive. And not just survive, but to live. She had far too many dreams and fantasies to live out yet. In fact, by her count, she had yet to live out even a single one of her dreams or fantasies. And now, thanks to the bodily collision between her and Sam, she had some tangibles to add to her fantasies. Not that she would be envisioning his particular shade of dark hair, strong jaw, and warm brown eyes. And she certainly wouldn't recall his unique scent of tea and whiskey, with a hint of sandalwood. The sandalwood part was added courtesy of the collision.

"If I had to," she flipped him a look, "I guess I would. But I'm not that desperate—and before you can counter that point, let me tell you, I am *not* that desperate."

"Nor will you be if you listen to your sister. She's a wise woman."

"This was your idea, Nobi?" Mimi found that hard to believe. Though Nobi wasn't cut from the same cloth as Mimi in terms of their competitive natures, Nobi had her own skills that she would never diminish. Mimi knew that with the utmost confidence.

But Nobi only nodded.

Well…that was shocking. "I'll think about it."

"Good—" Sam started to say in that rumbling deep voice of his.

"I have made no promises. I just said that I'll think about it."

And she would think about it. She planned to think about it. But that's all she would do with it. There was no way on God's green earth that she would ever consider playing small so another person could feel better about themselves and not be overshadowed by her.

"Do you want to be right or do you want to win?" The question struck her dead center in the heart. Her competitive nature balked at the idea that she couldn't have both. She wasn't naive enough to think that she was always right—just mostly right. And although she wasn't conceited enough to think she would always win (she did have Boudicca, Joan, and Zenobia for sisters after all), she was extremely confident—one might say—in her skill sets. But the fact that he would call her out and challenge her on such an intimate topic in front of others, rankled her.

"I can be both."

"Not always."

"Always." She almost bared her teeth to him and then decided to play nice. "I always get what I want."

She watched as he pulled his chin back at her words. Defensively? Conceding her point? Withdrawing from the argument? She wasn't sure.

And then, as if he was rethinking his previous gesture, he leaned in. Closer than she expected. His breath was so warm against her throat that when she swallowed she was quite sure the lump had to pass through his breath. He leaned in so closely in fact, that out of the corner of her eye Mimi saw Chris and Nobi discreetly lean in toward her as well. Ostensibly vying to hear what the man was about to say. She wasn't sure yet if she wanted them to hear it.

"Be careful with what you want, Mimi. You might just get it." Mimi clenched her thighs together for the second time in his presence. Her heart flopped around in her ribcage like a fish just pulled out of the water.

If she were always careful, that would have been the perfect rejoinder, but Mimi was not. So the next best reply was what flew out of her mouth in what she hoped was a steady stream but actually ended up just a touch more breathless than she would have wanted. "I'm not worried. I always know exactly what I want." And as she said those words, as true as they had been for the entirety of her life up until this point in time…she couldn't help notice the slight hiccup—the hesitation—in her breath.

She had always known exactly what she wanted. She knew what she wanted out of life, love, relationships. All of it. She knew what she wanted, and it was the fantasy. The fantasy. Her fantasies. Any of them. All of them. She wanted to be swept away. She wanted to nearly drown in her emotions, be carried away in the arms of a no-nonsense muscular man. A rogue. A rake. The one who would fall to his knees for her. She would be his world. He would die for her. If need be. She wanted fate to point out this man with the clarity of a diamond. With such reassurance, she would fight for her fantasy until her last breath.

And that's why she knew, she *really* did know, that Roger was that man. Fate had pointed him out. It had been one of the clearest signs she had ever interpreted in her life. They had literally been reaching for the same goals in life. And he wouldn't back down simply because she wanted the same thing. He knew what he wanted and he went after it. She was the same way. Fate had shown her that and she wouldn't let it go. The small issue of Roger being a little slow to the game was not really an issue. Time would fix that issue. She just knew it. She believed it with her whole beating heart.

The same heart that was currently transfixed in a rhythm that would not relent.

CHAPTER TEN

THE ARCHERY ACTIVITIES were about to start, and Mimi felt giddy at the prospect. This she was good at. And despite the conflicting advice she was receiving, she just knew in her heart that if she could show Roger her full self that he would accept her. And more. Fate had aligned the stars and shown her the brightest one. She just needed to stay the course.

This was no time to show fear, not that she ever did. She was fearless. Almost. There was only one thing she was afraid of—but, no, that rarely came up. She was always careful on that front. And her sister knew how to step in during those moments. They happened so infrequently that she had forgotten the last time one of her siblings had had to interfere on her behalf.

Mimi eyed the target. Casually, she let her eyes wander to Roger. Since her last dress hadn't caught his attention, she determined that perhaps that the man simply didn't have a proclivity to fashion-minded women. That wasn't a problem. Fashion wasn't a priority for her anyway. Roger was surveying the targets as well, and then his focus shifted to his equipment. His bow and arrows, that is. He was fastidiously checking the arrows, rubbing his fingers across each tip. It reminded her that she needed to check her bow soon, as well.

Roger walked toward her, and she wanted to clap. Perhaps he was already starting to see her differently.

"Sam," he tipped his head, gesturing toward the targets, "Are you ready for this?"

"Surprised you even have to ask," Sam chuckled. "I could hit these bullseyes blindfolded."

Mimi coughed, and Sam sent her a curious look. A knowing look. A look that made her want to laugh, rather than expose him.

Roger replied, "I'm sure you could—"

A sound wrenched the air, "Woof!"

Within a split second, Mimi saw black. Her feet grew roots. Her hands were submerged in pools of sweat. Her heart rattled inside of her, unsure of its place, and her thoughts scattered. They were running for the hills, exactly what she should be doing but couldn't.

There was nothing. But there was chaos. She could hear voices but the people around her were a blur. Where there had been trees, she only saw green blobs. Where there had been grass, she saw clumps of color. Not that she was even trying to look at the nature surrounding her. No, her sensations were dulled, yet somehow altogether heightened at the same time.

The hairs on her neck were standing to attention based on something she couldn't see. It was all reminiscent of a scene that she had tried to forget. In her everyday life, she had nearly forgotten it. But one sound. One small, yet petrifying sound reduced her to a weak little girl. If she had the emotional capacity for resentment in this instant, she would resent without any constraints, how fragile she felt. She was not fragile. But this…this feeling…caused by that one horrendous sound…she was exposed. Defenseless. Her body was already betraying her leaving her susceptible to another attack.

"Mimi?" That was Sam's voice, and it sounded laced with concern. A warm hand was on her forearm. "Are you all right?"

She couldn't answer him. She wanted to, but her tongue wouldn't cooperate with her. Never mind her tongue, her mind was working on repairing the damage of the explosion that had gone off in her brain. Pieces of memories were strewn about.

Visions of things that had never happened to her were intermingled. There were truths and there were falsehoods, but given an entire army to clean up this mess, it would still take her days to sift through and identify reality.

All she could see was a large, black dog barreling toward her. Terror would be putting it mildly. Her mind saw the dog but remembered another time and place. A large gray dog, snarling, baring its teeth. Lunging at her, plunging its teeth into her arm. A shriek.

Back in the blurry present, she heard Roger speak. "It's just a friendly dog."

Friendly? That's what the last owner had said. Mimi tried to open her eyes. Weren't they already open? She turned her head looking for Nobi. Nobi would know how to protect her. She knew what to do and how to guard her. It was irrational. She knew it. She knew it because she didn't know this dog, but it made her think of the other dog. And those words, *he's friendly*, they didn't reassure her. Not one bit. She had heard those words before but they weren't true. Nothing was true right now.

But her eyes watched as Roger casually stood at her side. Surely he would protect her. He would see her fear and do something. The dog was fast approaching, and she could feel tears yanking on her eyes, running toward her piping heart, but she couldn't move. Still couldn't speak. And then the oddest thing happened, Roger laughed. Not at her. She didn't think. But at the dog. It wasn't funny. Nothing was funny about this. Her throat was closing up, she couldn't breathe.

"What a good pup." Roger reached out his hand to pet the dog. The dog jumped up and Mimi shrieked. Her fists were clenched. But that was her last fully conscious thought, if that thought was even conscious. She couldn't determine.

Blackness.

An instant passed and all she could see was blackness. Yet despite the heaviness of her limbs, she knew she was still conscious. Blackness in front, but blue above. She looked down to check her feet. They were still rooted to the spot in the plush grass. When she brought her gaze back up, she realized that someone had stepped in front of her. Broad shoulders. A wall of protection. She was safe.

Her breath came back to her. She was in a safe place, safe from harm. There was someone willing to step in the gap and protect her. Someone other than her sisters or family. It was likely the smallest gesture to anyone else, but to her and her one fear, this man was a hero. This man, by merely standing in front of her as a wall, was making her world a better place. Or perhaps he was taking her to another place entirely. Another world. A place where there was peace and protection.

It had to be Roger. He had to have finally seen her terror and just stepped in front of her. He was kind and considerate like that. She could tell. As quiet as he was, he was the type of man to care. Being a gentleman, he would notice the needs of others and offer solutions to problems. His original tactic had probably been to make light of the situation and calm the dog, but once he saw her agony, he had obviously changed tactics. She was sure of it. As sure as she was about how fate had brought her to him in the first place. And this was the first of many sparkling moments for her and this protective man in front of her.

It had to be Roger, even though she wouldn't have noticed because the blurry present was only now starting to clear. He was her knight in shining armor. Yes, it was cliché. But she loved a good cliché. A good, strong, protective one at least.

What kind of man would he be if he didn't catch sight of her alarm?

A gentle presence was at her side, calm but bewildered. Not quite anxious, but concerned. For her. "Mimi," her sister asked, "are you all right?"

She turned her face to her sister, her body still too heavy to move, and she nodded. Stunned, yet working her mind and body free from the vise-like grip fear had on her. It was like waking up from a nightmare, the kind in which you tried to scream but couldn't. Her tongue felt thick and moving it took extra effort.

Finally the wall in front of her spoke, deep, authoritative. Commanding the dog to stay. And then with further instruction, Chris came into view replacing the man's firm but kind grip on the dog.

The wall turned. She eagerly looked up, awaiting Roger's golden eyes (they were golden, right?), anticipating the kindness of his face—

"Mimi," Sam's voice shook through her as though it were pounding against the drum of her heart. "Are you well?" The depth of concern in his voice confused her.

Sam?

He was the wall?

He was her protection?

He was her safe place?

God, above.

And then she really did see blackness, just after catching sight of the blue sky above.

She awoke in strong arms holding her, jostling her only slightly. "Where am I?" Her arms still felt weak, but at least her uncooperative tongue was functioning. It wasn't so thick anymore, and despite the dryness in her throat, she could manage the short question.

"Don't speak. Rest. I'm taking you back to the house." Sam spoke without even looking at her. There was no point in arguing, though she wasn't sure she even wanted to. With him, it was her default to contradict him. But here, next to him, in such a sensitive state, she didn't trust herself to refute him yet. She was still trying to process how she ended up on the ground. And why was he the one consoling her? Hadn't Roger protected her from the dog, her worst fear? No—the memory flooded her. It had all been Sam. The realization had caused her to swoon the first time.

She swooned? She had never swooned before. God, what was happening to her. If anything, she thought she would have fainted at the panic she felt at the sight of the dog, but afterward? It made no sense.

"I can walk," she lifted her arms to push herself out of his arms.

"Don't be so foolish."

With a dramatic sigh, she relented. Overexaggerating the sigh of course. She couldn't let him know that she was actually relieved. Her arms felt like lead. If she had pushed herself free of his arms, she was pretty sure she would have landed like a pile of pudding on the ground. And really, he didn't need to see her in a pile of dirt. Again.

She gripped the reins on the smirk dying to go wild on her face. It wasn't so bad being carried. Not that being carried by him in particular was satisfying. But the way his arms fit around her body, conveying his strength and determination wasn't a bad thing. And though it wasn't anything to write her sister Boudicca about, it wasn't entirely unnoticeable how his chest rippled when he shifted her weight ever so slightly. And the way he stared straight ahead, not giving a passing glance to any distractions meant less that he wasn't a force to be reckoned with and more that when he wanted to get something done, he did it.

Another sigh blew past her lips.

"Do you need to stop and rest?" He stood still for a moment, awaiting her answer. And while he waited, he tilted his chin to study her eyes.

"I should be asking you that. You're the one carrying the heavy load."

"I'm fine. You weigh nothing."

"Not nothing," she replied defiantly.

He cocked a brow at her. "Really? You want to argue about that?"

"I'm just stating a fact."

His gaze penetrated her face for a beat or two while she stared off into the clouds. It was stupid to argue about her weight, but she wasn't going to relent. It was true. She didn't weigh *nothing*. She had substance to her. So yes, she did want to argue about it. For some odd reason it felt as though by arguing that incontrovertible truth she was able to cling to some semblance of reality that existed before everything turned upside down.

Sam was being nice to her? He was protecting her? That was why she swooned. Not because she was dizzy, but because the entire world had tilted on its axis and her feet hadn't been able to keep up with the rotation. Never mind that everyone else had been able to, that was clearly beside the point.

"If you can argue about that, then I think you're fine to head to the house." His arms shifted and she could feel him about to put her down. Her body rejected that notion.

For a fleeting moment insanity took over (or really, just her flare for the dramatics), and she rattled out a heavy sigh. "I…uh…don't know if I'm quite ready for that far of a walk." His dubious stare made her uncomfortable to the point that she added, "Of course, I could do it. Just…erm…slowly." Her chest constricted, awaiting his reply. She would have liked to shoo off the elephant that had plopped down right there on her bodice, for at that exact moment, her corset needed to be loosened not tightened.

"It's fine. I'll carry you."

And as she let out a small breath she hadn't realized she was holding, she thought she saw a small smirk line the corner of his mouth while he stepped forward.

CHAPTER ELEVEN

After that morning, Sam needed a quiet walk in the garden. His body was charged and he needed a few minutes of peace. Mimi being afraid—no, terrified—of dogs was playing in his mind. She was a strong, independent woman. It was odd to think of her having a weakness that debilitated her.

As he strode down one of the more isolated paths, he heard an odd sound.

A grunt.

He moved closer to the rose bush blocking his view. He was pretty sure there was a stone bench on the other side. The perfect place for an assignation, but who would be doing that in the middle of the day? Joan and James most likely. Reassuring himself that nothing was amiss, he was about to turn when he heard the voice more clearly this time.

"Right there…" came the tight plea.

But that was not the voice of Joan. And he knew that not because he knew Joan's voice so well, but because he knew Mimi's voice, and this was hers.

He moved even closer to the rose bush. What the hell was she doing? And who was she with? She was obviously over the dog incident, thankfully.

"God, why are you so hard?" her voice complained on a small whimper that sent a jolt straight to his cock. She shouldn't be saying those things to anyone else. No, she shouldn't be saying those things to anyone at all.

He didn't want to be listening to this. He shouldn't be eavesdropping. She almost sounded like she was in pain, but then again, there was a fine line between pain and pleasure.

"Just a little bit further…" Her voice was now settling itself into his bones. His muscles were involuntarily twitching in ways he needed to stifle.

"Bend…"

Bend? What the hell was she doing? And with whom? There was a burning rage…an inferno of fury that was simmering, about to explode. Unleash on the man she was with. Likely that addlepated idiot Roger. Boring, bland Roger. The bacon brain hadn't even noticed her fear of dogs. He had played it off as some kind of dislike, or perhaps he hadn't even recognized anything was amiss. He had actually encouraged the dog to play, but based on Mimi's eyes, a dog playing, and a dog attacking weren't different things to her. He had been the one to step in. Thank God he did. He was pretty sure he had prevented Mimi from a mortifying experience, at least, more mortifying than it was. But then when he turned around she had swooned? What the deuce was that about?

"Yes! There it is." Pleasure riddled her tone and addled his brain.

This woman was an innocent and he was overhearing her in the throes of passion, albeit slightly odd phrases. But who was he to judge?

He really shouldn't interrupt this. Then again, he really should. He had to. This woman couldn't keep herself out of trouble.

Sam rushed around the bushes fighting all ten steps as to whether he should march in with eyes open or not. But as he always did in life, he chose eyes wide open.

"Mimi, I must insist you stop—"

"Sam?" Mimi's eyes flew up to what he could only assume was a disheveled appearance. Upon choosing eyes wide open, he had decided that raking his hands through his hair five times was necessary, as well as loosening his cravat slightly. It had grown deucedly more difficult to breathe with each step that brought him closer to her.

A clatter caught his attention. Her bow dropped to the courtyard floor.

His eyes flickered around. She was alone. With her bow. Nothing was amiss. Except her heaving bosom, which, really, he couldn't help but notice since her breaths were so short and shallow, thus causing a slight jiggle in places where he really shouldn't be looking, and causing a rambling in his brain where order normally reigned. "Wh-what are you doing?"

"I'm restringing my bow." Her brows furrowed. "Should I stop?"

"N-no." He shook his head.

"You don't just get to barge into my life and take over, telling me what to do and what not to do. I'll restring my bow wherever I damn well want to."

"Yes, of course." Her response, part of it made perfect sense. Certainly, the woman could restring her bow wherever she wanted to, so long as it wasn't a euphemism for something else. But the part about him barging in on her life? As if that was something he did often. That part made no sense. What was she upset about? Hadn't he just offered her protection in more than one way? Couldn't she just be grateful? This woman was driving him to drink.

SHE DIDN'T NEED it, she kept telling herself, but she took a nap after everything that had taken place that morning. The incident with the dog had left her shaken on so many levels, and she had tried to regain her equilibrium by focusing on a task she loved and knew could absorb her full attention. Only to be interrupted by Sam. He was everywhere, upsetting everything. So yes, she probably did need a nap actually.

Before all the events of the evening could take place, Mimi didn't see any harm in resting her head a little. Perhaps her pride a little as well. But mostly her heart. If only she had known what kind of dreams would visit her in her short repose, she might not have been so quick to toss her tresses on the pillow. Then again…she may have chosen to do so for a longer period of time.

And now as she sat running a brush through her hair, she could no more prevent the thoughts of the dreams from entering her mind than she could stop air from entering her body.

It had been so vivid. They had been on a beach. She was wading in the water, watching a storm approach. A voice shouted at her, and she promptly ignored it. The shouting continued until the body was right beside her and she could no longer pretend at anything. He asked her what she was doing here, but she gave him no reply. With closed eyes, she faced the water, letting the waves lap at her feet. The water was cool, refreshing. She waded deeper into the receding waters.

She remembered what came next as if it had been a reality. A growl and a sudden move. Strong arms. A warm body.

She couldn't finish the thought as the memory produced a shiver up Mimi's spine. Her grip on the brush tightened so that she didn't drop it.

Back on the beach, she saw the dream in the mirror. Sam threw her over his shoulder and hauled her back to the sand. He was reprimanding her, though she didn't know what for. His voice was harsh, yet it was washing over her like the waves, tickling her feet.

He stopped. Placed her on the ground, but the momentum had caused her to stumble back. In an effort to regain her balance, she reached for him but only managed to grip his shirt. Not expecting her quick movements, he tumbled down with her. His arms bracketed her on either side, his weight inches above her. But her body was aching to feel his heaviness now that she knew what he felt like. She wanted to feel the weight of him, the strength of him, the man-ness of him, all over her.

The image in the mirror was blurry, her eyes stung. The ache between her legs. The tremble in her hand. Her lips parted. Just as she had felt upon waking immediately, now again, she wanted to touch herself—

KNOCK. KNOCK. KNOCK.

The brush clattered down on the table.

"Mimi," Nobi's voice rang out, "are you ready for this evening?"

Her sister entered the room, Mimi was too stunned to approach her. She needed a moment to collect herself.

Nobi gasped. "You're not even dressed."

Mimi shook her head. The nap was supposed to have offered her a reset; instead it only further confused her. "I didn't know which dress to choose." That was true. What she didn't offer up was the reason for her indecision. Which color, which style, which cut would look best on her? Normally she would answer that for herself. Whatever she wanted to wear she would wear. There was no question of impressing someone else. For the first time ever, only the other night, she had chosen a dress for someone else. She had hoped to capture Roger's attention. At the time she had wanted to prove to herself that she could do it (wear a scandalous dress) and get what she wanted (Roger pledging his undying love for her).

But tonight…tonight when she was about to pick out a dress, she stopped herself. For the first time, as she grazed her finger along the satin dresses, she wanted to know what someone else might think about her. It wasn't about herself or impressing anyone. It was about one man's true opinion of her. And she wanted it to count. She wanted…she took a deep breath in…she wanted him to see her. Fully. That meant seeing past the dress.

But that was the vexing part of it all. Roger was her destiny. Fate had pointed him out. Yet…every encounter since the store had not lived up to her expectations. If fate was handing her her future, shouldn't love be blossoming?

"Mimi, did you hear me? I asked you what you are going to wear."

"I don't know." She felt a bit dazed. From the afternoon. From the dream. From the realization about her wardrobe.

"This isn't like you. Are you all right?"

"Which dress do you think suits me best?" Mimi asked her sister.

Nobi crouched in front of her, meeting her eyes. "I think you suits you best. Just be yourself, dear sister. Don't worry about what's on the outside. It doesn't matter. It has never mattered to you. Why should it now?"

Because my future is on the line. Because love is on the line. Because my life is hanging in the balance of this decision. Was what she wanted to say...but she couldn't. It sounded too vulnerable for the moment.

"It shouldn't matter, should it?"

Nobi shook her head.

"It doesn't matter." She stood up, and speaking more to herself than Nobi, she added, "If he likes me, he likes me. And he'll like me no matter what I wear. It's not about what's on the outside. I need to be me and accept my fate."

There was that word. That all-consuming, all-vexing, altogether loop-throwing word. But she would handle fate later.

Now, she needed to dress.

IT WASN'T THE dress. Sam kept telling himself that. It wasn't the pale pink against her snow-colored skin. It wasn't the femininity of the colors and the cut that draped itself down her bosom and around her waist. And it wasn't just the way she moved with grace and intention. It was the woman underneath the dress. Sam bit the inside of his cheek, tempering the groan that clawed at his throat.

Her in his arms. Her against his body. Her fear. Subsiding.

Something had tethered itself between them, and he resented every inch of that rope.

Mimi stood in front of Roger. Damn him. Moving her soft pink lips. Laughing. The sound laced through him, compelling him to take a step toward her. He needed to stay away. He needed a distraction.

Thank God one had come in the form of a letter this afternoon after the swooning event. His cousin had arrived and was making himself at home, and Sam was only too grateful to have his most treasured possession at Chris's house in his hidden safe. Chris, the man of secrets. It only made sense that he had a hidden dungeon with a hidden safe and a hidden access code. It was the reason Sam had left his possessions with him rather than risking leaving them at his own house.

Speaking of the sneaky (but trustworthy) bastard, Chris sauntered up. "You look like you're about to call him out."

"You must have mistaken me for my father," Sam ground out. His father had called out one too many duels, ultimately resulting in his untimely death. Though, could one call it untimely when a man had engaged in over a dozen duels?

Chris took a sip and stared at Mimi and Roger over the rim of his glass. "Not sure how I could mistake you for him. You're nothing like him."

"Truly, that's the nicest thing anyone has ever said to me." Sam's heart flopped over at the compliment. Usually he wasn't one to get twisted up in emotions, but there were too many flying about his head, like flies hovering around a pile of cow dung, for him to keep his distance. He had to swat at least one of them. And Chris's fly was the one.

"I'm sure I've said it before."

"I would remember."

"Well," Chris slapped him on the back. "Perhaps it's just too obvious then. No one wants to be the one to state the obvious."

Sam just grunted in reply. He wasn't sure he could trust his words. Was it true that no one equated him to his father? It seemed unlikely, but he was hopeful, given how much time he spent trying to remake a name and an image for himself.

"You think people should state the obvious more often then?" The only thing Sam could see was Chris's profile, so he couldn't fully decipher the expression he wore.

"I think people should say what they want to say."

Chris turned to face him. "Are you sure?"

"Yes." Sam's eyes were on Chris and Mimi simultaneously. Chris was calm, shoulders relaxed, and a little smirk toyed with the corner of his mouth. Mimi was laughing louder than was probably necessary, given Roger's blank expression and Nobi's curious face. What the deuce was so funny over there? Was she trying a new tactic to secure Roger's attention?

Chris's eyes narrowed while he raised his glass to his mouth. A slow sip and swallow, followed by a repeated inquiry. "Are you sure?"

"Damn it, man. Of course, I'm sure." Sam raked his hands through his hair as he watched Mimi's hand land on Roger's forearm. Fire pulsed through his own arm. Demanding. "If I didn't mean it, I wouldn't say it. And if you mean something you should say it." Chris gave him a quizzical expression, but Sam wasn't finished with his little rant. "Say what you want. Obvious or not. Perhaps it's not as clear as one might think."

"Perhaps."

Silence filled the space between them for a beat before Chris continued. "Perhaps…I had more faith in you. I thought you were the most intelligent of us all."

Sam scoffed. Mimi's fingers were touching her lips. Covering a laugh now? That was new. Or wiping a few droplets of her drink from her mouth?

"Ah…so you think so too?" Chris asked.

"Well, I didn't say it."

Chris chuckled. "We may be in agreement, but that doesn't make us both right. I'm rethinking my assessment of your intelligence."

Sam could feel the blood boiling in his system. What was Mimi doing now? She was standing far too close to Roger. Nobi should say something. Someone should say something. It was obvious what was happening. He would just have to be the one to step up and take action before something truly scandalous could happen.

"If you'll excuse me," he started to say to Chris.

"Oh. I think I'll join you for this," Chris said, suppressing a cough.

Chapter Twelve

"A toast," Jacob lifted his hand in the air as Sally stood smiling at his side, "to my bride. I never saw love like this coming, but now I can't unsee it. You are my everything. I can't live without you." His voice was quiet, it didn't boom throughout the room, but his statements were bold. "To my bride, may she always feel loved and treasured, and because her happiness is mine, may her joy never cease."

Sam watched and followed suit as the guests raised their glasses and toasted the bride. It was a little (or a lot) over the top for Sam's preference—a man's happiness shouldn't depend on a woman—but he drank in support of his friends anyway.

And even though his body was facing the bride and groom, his eyes were still watching Mimi's movements. He hadn't been able to reach her before the toast started. Now she was clinking glasses with Roger. He studied her as she smiled, and took a sip. Could she be any more obvious? And oblivious?

The toast was over. Glasses were being placed on trays carried by footmen that had flooded the room. Now it was time to take action and save Mimi from herself.

As he moved toward her, Chris fell in step behind him.

"You're actually following me?"

"I wouldn't miss it."

"She's not going to like what I have to say."

"Has she ever?"

"True." Sam mulled over that thought. It felt like he was swallowing gravel as he let it sink in.

"Don't embarrass her, Sam."

"I wouldn't. I plan on speaking to her alone."

Chris raised an eyebrow at that notion, questioning him and his judgment, and he didn't like it. "How do you plan on doing that exactly?"

"I have my ways."

"I know your ways, Sam."

"Not like that. She's a lady. I'm trying to protect her reputation not seal her fate in scandal."

"Are you sure?"

Sam stopped abruptly and Chris's shoulder bumped into him. The two men looked each other in the eyes. "Yes," Sam ground out between his clenched teeth, "I'm very sure. I have no use for a young, naive girl like Mimi. Too many opinions. Too much drama. Too many dreams." And then as an afterthought that really shouldn't have been an afterthought, he added, "Besides, you know I'm not looking for a wife."

"Yes. I do vaguely recall you uttering that vow. Not sure why though."

Sam scoffed. "You don't know why?" He stalled for time by repeating his confusion cloaked in disbelief. "You don't know why? Need I remind you of my father?"

"Need I remind you that you're not him?"

"This is too much in one evening, Chris. Leave the subject alone. I'm not marrying. She's too naive, yet too independent. We would fight all the time."

"So you've thought about it?"

Had he? The question shocked him. He had pictured Mimi in a few ways. And seeing them arguing about a silly game or competing against each other for another win...he couldn't remember if he had actually envisioned a future with her. That would be odd. "She's not for me."

"No. She's not." Chris pointed toward Mimi and Roger. "Apparently she's for him."

The statement labeling Mimi as another man's belonging cut his airway off. He coughed to gain some oxygen.

There was no more time to chat. With Chris. He needed to talk with Mimi, and that boring bland Roger was not going to stand in his way.

A few more strides and Sam was right in front of Mimi and her vexatious dress that screamed gentle femininity even though he knew the body beneath it was a competitive hellion. Before he could speak, his throat ran dry while he glared at Mimi. It took two quick swallows and Chris inserting himself in the conversation before Sam actually spoke.

"Excuse me, Mimi." Her eyes lazily drew up from his waist (or lower?) and as they fell on his lips, he realized he didn't have a plan as to how he would get her alone without alerting the guests of his intentions. Ahem—intentions he didn't actually have.

Chris cleared his throat, side-eyeing Sam. "Roger, Zenobia, might I interest you in a game of piquet."

"I'd love to join you," Mimi chimed in.

"Unfortunately, we already have a fourth." Sam knew it pained Chris to utter that prevarication, and he would owe the man later for his discreet, if not a touch awkward, approach to helping him out.

Mimi's eyes drilled into Chris, but he wasn't watching. Smart man. Chris's attention was all on Zenobia, as if a silent conversation was happening between them.

And while Mimi watched Chris, and Chris watched Zenobia, and Roger, well, he wasn't really looking at anything in particular, Sam studied Mimi and her movements. Her shoulders were thrown back and her lips tightened into a straight line. He wasn't sure how much time he would have with her before she turned on her heel and left him alone to nurture his drink, so he would have to be direct.

Nobi patted her sister's arm and whispered something inaudible. The moment the three left him alone with Mimi, he didn't waste a second.

"What are you doing?" Sam threw at her.

"I was talking."

"You were doing more than talking."

Mimi huffed and blinked hard. "It's not as though I kissed the man in front of everyone."

"I would hope not." Red. Flashes of red flogged his eyes, and a burning sensation prickled his chest. As if someone had found random bits of kindling around his ribcage and gathered them in one spot in hopes of building a fire. Kindling he was neither aware of nor needed. And a fire he neither wanted nor understood.

"I would never allow my first kiss to be in public."

First? She had yet to be kissed. He knew she was an innocent. She was far too naive to be anything but an innocent, yet never to have been kissed…The kindling around his chest had garnered a spark and the spark caught fire. As he studied her lips—pink and full—they parted, and his chest rose in a deep inhale. He could imagine himself leaning in and introducing her lips to his. Giving her her first kiss. What the devil was wrong with him? How many drinks had he imbibed this evening?

He banished the vision and berated her. That had been the plan. He needed to stick to it.

"You shouldn't be kissing at all."

She stuck out her chin. "Don't be so old, Sam."

"Don't be so young," he returned. It was the best he could come up with in the moment.

She laughed at that. But it wasn't a laugh he could join in on. It was the kind of laugh a woman produced when she knew she had the upper hand.

Damn.

His face was heating up and his fists were clenched at his side while her eyes were darting around the room looking for an escape. But he needed more time to tell her to stop being a fool.

"Come with me," he said.

"I think I'll join my sister—"

"Now." He caught her eye and intensified his gaze.

"Sam, really." She had started to plead, but he had already taken her hand on his forearm with the appearance of taking a jaunt around the room. Of course, the plan would be to secure more privacy than that.

"Don't make a scene, Mimi."

She sighed, whether in acquiescence or not, he couldn't be sure; he was too focused on his goal.

There was a door leading outside. He took a quick glance around and stepped through the frame with her.

"Sam, I must insist—"

But because no one could see them now, he hauled her up on his shoulder and took her down the steps into the garden.

"I'll scream," she threatened.

"If you were going to scream, you would have already done so. Besides, you wouldn't actually follow through. That would cause a scandal with results you wouldn't be too keen on."

He could tell that she clamped her mouth shut because her arms had crossed and were banging against his lower back as he trod on the grass finding a secluded spot. She kicked her legs a few times, but it was all for display.

Finally, he found a spot hidden away and dropped her to the ground.

"What are you doing? Don't even think about kissing me." She rolled her lips inward and placed her hands on her hips.

"I'm not trying to seduce you, Mimi. I'm preventing you from making a fool of yourself in front of Roger. Again."

"It's none of your business how I conduct myself with him."

"Like hell it isn't. Where's your father? What are your sisters doing? Why is no one protecting you?"

"My father is busy. Traveling. As usual. My sisters are busy. Married or getting there. And I don't need protecting. I can protect myself. Now, get out of my way." She shoved at his chest, but he didn't budge. Well, most of his body didn't budge. And if one didn't count the slight swelling between his legs, then really, his whole body was preternaturally still.

"Move, Sam."

"Not until we talk." Talk. That's all he wanted to do. He had to remind himself.

"What do we have to talk about?"

He scratched his jaw. Another gesture to buy himself time. But in this instance he needed time to first calm the throb of his cock.

Mimi filled the silence, answering her own question. "You know this is the third time you have hauled me out of a place?"

It was probably best that she brought up the topic of conversation, as he couldn't think in quite the straight line he normally was quite capable of doing. But wait, three hauls? Perhaps she wasn't thinking right. "Three? I think not."

"Three!" She pulled her hands free from the crisscross they had been entangled in, and started counting on her fingers. "Right now. The archery. And the beach—"

"The beach. No. Wasn't me." He gripped his bicep. Tightly. "Must be your other beau." He didn't want to imagine another man touching Mimi. Never mind hauling her over his shoulder so that her breasts bounced against his back.

"Other beau?"

"You know what I mean."

"I don't know what you mean."

"I don't think you know what *you* mean. I haven't hauled you out three times." He needed to regain control of the conversation. And somehow regaining control of the conversation entailed him inching closer and closer to her. They were toe to toe. Mere inches from each other. Her head barely reaching his shoulders.

"Two or three? What does it matter? It's one or two too many." The puff of her huff was warm on his jaw, feeling less like ire and more like fire.

Damn her. This woman was vexing beyond belief. If he wasn't absolutely certain he was sane, he would feel lost in her logic. "Wait. Is it *one* or *two* too many?"

"What?" Her face was flushed, he could see it in the light of the moon. And her eyelids were floating at half-mast. She was enigma at its finest. If he didn't know better he'd have said she wanted to kiss him, all while he wanted to squeeze his hand into a fist, until he realized it was resting on her hip, pulling her closer to his own heat.

Though he needed an answer to his question, his throat worked hard, rendering his vocal chords useless. Finally, his voice came out raspy. "Well…if it's one too many, that means one was…acceptable. If it was two too many that means neither time was desirable. I would just like to know which it is."

"Why?"

Well, that he couldn't answer. Mostly because he wasn't willing to admit why even to himself. "No reason other than to lord it over you."

Her chin tipped up at him, lips parted, like she was about to press up on her tiptoes and make contact with him. She would do that. But she would be the kind to do that for one of two reasons: one, she wanted to kiss him or two, she wanted to shut him up.

Softly, her hand pressed into his chest, where a rabid animal was loosed behind the cage. And just when he was sure that she was going to kiss him, before he could figure out what his response was going to be to that, she turned him on his head.

A low growl escaped her mouth. "You are the worst gentleman I have ever met."

Hand tightening around her waist, he growled back, "Well, perhaps it doesn't signify, anyway. The way things are going, it won't be the last time I haul you somewhere."

CHAPTER THIRTEEN

IF SAM THOUGHT the wedding toast had been saccharine, going through a rehearsal of the ceremony was that much more agonizing. Sally was standing at the end of the aisle looking out over the church, pondering who knew what. The flowers cascading over the pews? The fabric draped overhead? The lit candles at the front?

Her face was scrunched up as if the number of wrinkles produced correlated to the amount of stress she was facing. James and Joan weren't much help, since they were essentially staring into each other's eyes in the corner, possibly looking for a quick escape. They had hardly been around this house party, but being newly engaged, Sam didn't need to ask why that was so.

As he watched Mimi walk toward Sally, he had a weighted feeling, much like a large rock, slowly sinking to his feet. This couldn't be good. Mimi was not known for her good ideas. Though he was one to speak. Last night, hauling her into the garden hadn't exactly been one of his better ideas. After he scolded her, he stared at her wondering what to do next. Thankfully she had just turned on her heel and stormed back into the ballroom. Otherwise, he wasn't too sure what he would have done.

That night his dreams had kept him awake, though he couldn't recall (or admit) what (or who) had been the object of his feral desire. It certainly wasn't the blonde hellion at the back of the abbey talking to Sally.

That large rock inside of him was still on a slow descent as he studied the two women speaking, but it was too much like deciphering a foreign language. Hands were moving, a few pats on the shoulder, a swipe under the eyes, a few laughs, a scowl directed at someone near the front of the church (Sam didn't bother verifying who), and then a few more laughs. Sally was gesticulating with her hands, and Mimi was nodding. Her face froze for an instant. Coincidentally, it was the same instant that the rock in Sam's body hit the floor.

Her eyes met his, and even from where he was standing, he could see her tighten her lips and pull them back into a smile. Another nod and then Sally was walking toward him.

She was shining with happiness. This was really not going to be good.

"Sam," she was almost breathless in her delight, "good news." Only, he knew it wasn't. "Mimi has proposed the most perfect suggestion." She clapped her hands. "I was having the most difficult time envisioning everything only moments ago."

Only moments ago, Sam had watched her struggle. He only hoped her newfound peace didn't require anything absurd from him. But really, from the gleam in her eye, and the frozen face Mimi had sent his way, he knew that something was about to be requested of him.

"Since I'm the bride," she beamed, "I couldn't see everything from the outside. Mimi," she gestured toward the innocent-looking-but-not-so-innocent being in question, "has agreed to take my place in the ceremony so I can watch everything unfold and make certain it's everything I have ever dreamed it should be."

A reply of some kind was expected of him at this point. He offered a low hum that he hoped conveyed support more than caution.

"But I couldn't have her walk down the aisle to Jacob." She laughed. And he wanted to laugh too because by this point he knew what the request was.

"Yes. That would be silly."

"Of course it would be. He's not her fiancé."

Sam withheld from stating the obvious. That he was also in fact, not her (or anyone's) fiancé.

"Besides, I wanted Jacob at my side so we can discuss everything."

Sam already knew that Jacob would just agree with everything that Sally wanted. The man was smitten. More than smitten. The man was floating around on a love cloud that no one else could see or touch.

"Makes sense," Sam mumbled.

"I knew you would see it my way." Had he another choice? Not with a bride.

"So you'll stand right over here." She gently (but firmly) pushed his forearm to guide him into his spot. The spot. The spot that wasn't his. Shouldn't be his. Would never be his. But somehow was his.

Inwardly he groaned and closed his eyes for a moment. He wanted to rake his hands through his hair and clench his fists, but then settled on scrubbing the lower half of his face with a long blink.

He was going to have to watch Mimi walk down the aisle. Oh, he had been prepared for that. Her as the bridesmaid, him as the groomsman. It meant nothing. But now, to be the stand-in groom and her the bride? It was too much.

He didn't need to envision her in white walking toward him, ready and willing to give him everything. Her life. Her mind. Her body. Obviously, that's not what was happening. He didn't need to think those thoughts.

"Everyone ready?" Sally shouted. Who needed to be ready? It was Mimi and Sam that had the bulk of the work.

After moving to a spot at the perimeter of the room with Jacob, Sally called out, "Sam? Are you ready?"

A nod confirmed his state of readiness, which was to say, he was as ready as he was going to ever be pretending to be a groom to a woman he couldn't have but was for some reason of late burning to have.

"Begin!" Sally boomed. Mimi started to take a few steps down the aisle, and Sam averted his eyes, paying special attention to the paintings on the wall and then the meticulously painted stained glass windows.

"Stop!" Sally quickly called out and rushed over to Sam. "You must watch the bride. You don't have to be in love with her—"

"I'm not."

Sally's eyes widened at his interruption but she quickly schooled her features. "No, of course. Just face her and watch her walk down the aisle." A quick pat on his head as if he were a child in need of encouragement to brush his teeth, she walked away.

Sam forced himself to look up at Mimi. She must be feeling as awkward as him because she had a goofy grin on her face and she sent him a wink. Well, so long as she felt nothing, he could feel nothing. His lips loosened, not into a smile exactly, but at least not into a scowl any longer. He was pretty sure he had a nice resting face of contentment.

Mimi had taken about ten steps when Sally bellowed, "Stop!"

What the deuce was it this time?

Sally's eyes were darting around the room until she found what she was looking for. With something white and fluffy in her hands, she skipped over to Mimi. Sally's body was blocking Sam's view, so he couldn't see what the mad woman was doing. When she stepped away, his heart stopped for a second.

Mimi's face was covered in a veil and her hands were holding her flowers. He couldn't see her teasing smile anymore, but for some reason he didn't sense that she was as playful as she had been moments ago.

Her gait had slowed and her feet moved with great intention. Toward him.

Inexplicably, his heart was struggling to pound out its normal rhythm. In its place, his pulse beat an erratic pattern.

When she stood in front of him, he reached out his hand and she took it. Standing before him, he studied her face through the veil. This was what nearly every man did. It was a milestone in a man's life to get married. Nearly every man would search for, claim, and marry a wife. He would devote himself to her wellbeing, she to his, and they would unite their souls together before God. He had never once in his life considered doing that. He knew what love did to a man. Especially to the men of his family. He didn't want the craziness, the dependency, the impulsiveness that came with love.

Yet, here…in these moments…watching Mimi walk toward him…he couldn't shake the koala of emotions that was clinging to him as if he were a tree.

He needed to see her face. See what she was thinking.

He reached forward and lifted the veil.

His breathing stuttered as he looked into her eyes. The depths of her eyes led straight to her soul. She was a hellion. Nothing in life would be easy with her. But when she committed to something, she gave her all. What would it be like for her to give her all to him?

Her tongue dragged along her lower lip as she looked up at him under dark lashes. She was teasing him. Did she know it?

That plump lower lip of hers was begging to be sucked on. Her fingers were born to explore, and he wanted them to start on his body. He could picture her underneath him. Hell, he didn't need to picture it. He had experienced it. He had felt her pliable body beneath him, and he wanted to have those sensations again. With more permission.

His hands wanted to introduce her to pleasure. She was a virgin, and he still wanted to give her untold delight. He could feel his tongue growing thick, anticipating what she might taste like. Her legs would open wide for him and his light stubble would graze her inner thighs. He would spread her lower lips and suck from the fount that was her.

He wanted to plunge into her and touch her in places that no man ever had. He wanted to see her eyes fall shut and her mouth fall open when he made her come. Calling his name. Oh, she would scream his name multiple times before he would let up. And he knew she would be loud. He could read it in her eyes.

Once he had her begging for more, he would cease his ministrations until he heard her sobbing, felt her thrusting, for more. He wouldn't let her off easily. The same way she never let anyone get away with anything. No, she would be his in the bedroom. Even if he had to tie her there. She needed someone to show her the realities of life, and he wanted to be the one to do it. The one. The one and only. And that was the most alarming part of his thoughts.

"Sam?" One whispered word from her shook all his visions loose. Unfortunately, that one word hadn't caused them to disappear. No. They had been loosed, and now they wanted to run free.

This was trouble.

CHAPTER FOURTEEN

LATER THAT EVENING, Mimi was still shaking from the intensity of Sam's gaze during the rehearsal. It was if she could feel him inside of her, just from the look he had given her. She rubbed her legs together, the same move she had done at least once every minute since the ceremony. She ached there. She needed relief. But her heart was troubled.

If Sam could make her feel this way without doing anything, she was desperate to know how Roger could make her feel.

But every time she thought of Roger, the quickening in her heart slowed. And she didn't want to feel the normal pace of her heart right now. She wanted Sam's eyes grazing her body again. More than that. She wanted to feel him on top of her.

God, she needed relief. She had time before the evening's events started. Quickly she made up her mind, ran to her door and locked it, then threw herself under her coverlet.

Her body was thrumming with need as she pressed her breasts into the mattress. The friction lit up her body with sparks. She pulled up her skirts and guided her hand down to her center. God, she was so wet. She had never felt so wet before. Her finger easily slid between her folds. Her slit throbbed in appreciation as her fingers played and glided. She was coiled so tightly that she knew she would find relief quickly. Her fingers tapped up to her pearl and started moving in circles.

She remembered his weight on her body. His arms wrapped

around her, carrying her. Feeling the fullness of his chest. Even through his layers, she could sense his strength. And then she came back to his smoldering eyes during the ceremony, watching her. Hungry for her, though she knew that was impossible. She didn't care if it wasn't true. She let his eyes call to her, reach through her, and pull her release from her. She muffled her cry in the mattress. Whether she called Sam's name or God's name, she wasn't sure. She didn't even want to think about it.

With limp arms and a breath ratcheting through her, she lay in her bed until she regained her equilibrium, but even after her breath had returned to normal, and her arms felt their usual weight, she wasn't quite sure she had regained that elusive equanimity she desired.

A few hours later, standing in the drawing room, Mimi was irritated. At herself. At fate. At Sam. At Roger. Life. Love. The glass of ratafia in her hands. Anything and everything. But most importantly, she needed answers. She hadn't gotten drunk (ahem—tipsy) since the night she suggested to her sisters that they do the duke dare in the first place. But tonight seemed as good a night as any for a repeat. No one would miss her with all the activities going on, so she slipped out of the room in search of some whiskey. Like any good man, she was pretty sure she could find some in Sally's father's library. Undoubtedly, a bottle would be hidden behind some books or in a cupboard.

Sure enough, within a minute of her search, Mimi found a bottle and poured a generous helping in her glass. She wasn't sure if she was on cup three or four when Roger walked in, but it was about time.

She hiccupped. "About time you arrived." Had she already said that? The curious expression on his face indicated confusion.

"Me?" Roger asked, pointing to his own chest. As if he would ask *me* and point to another person's chest. She giggled at the thought.

"Are you all right, Mimi?"

"Yes," she pushed herself up from the armchair she just realized she was sitting in. "I'm perfectly gell...erm...well."

"I'll go get your sister."

Oh what a boring thing to do.

"What's that?"

Did she say that aloud?

"Yes, you did." Roger looked at her blandly.

This was getting to be too much. Mimi opened her mouth and intentionally produced some words. "I'm in need of some answers." This was her chance. She was drunk. She could appreciate that fact now. But she still needed answers, and this was a good way to get them. Absolutely nothing wrong with this method. Fate told her that Roger was her destiny. Experience was refuting fate. Now she needed to know how Roger could make her feel. She stood and ambled over toward him.

"I just—erm—came in for a book. I should go."

"No," she said a little too loudly as she waved her arm out to the side showing off the room. "Stay. Sit." She tried to push him down onto the settee. The man didn't move. He was built quite sturdy. Not as broad and muscular as Sam, but still. No one was really like Sam, were they?

"I must insist—"

"What the hell is going on here?" That voice sounded an awful like Sam if he were to barge in on them and use his whisper shouting voice.

"Sam." Roger stepped back from her, and she almost lost her balance but Sam caught her around her waist.

"What are you doing?" Sam blasted Roger.

"I came in for a book, and she was here already three sheets to the wind."

"What are you going to do about it?"

At this particular moment, Mimi wished her eyes weren't so glossy because she really would like to see the glances passing between the two men. Pfft. She didn't need to see them. She knew what they would be. Roger with his imperviously bland look and Sam with his intense death stare.

But this was the moment Roger could step up. They had been caught in a scandalous moment together. This was fate. This was fate's method and she didn't even know it. Roger would speak up and offer his protection. Love was to come after marriage. That must be it—

"Nothing," Roger answered. "I'm not going to do anything. And I suggest you see her to her room before anything else happens."

And then he was gone. And fate…what the hell was fate's problem? Didn't she know how to pick the right man for her? This was not going according to plan.

"Let's go," Sam said gruffly.

"No." She didn't want to go anywhere. Not with him or anyone. She needed time to let the haze clear so she could process the absurdity that was fate.

"I said, let's go. We're leaving now."

"I'm not going anywhere with you, y-you …ogre."

"I didn't ask. I'm telling you that we're leaving," he growled.

"Oh no. Now I'm scared." She meant to say it in a taunting tone but she ended up giggling. Sam was so ridiculous. If he thought he could scare her, he had another thing coming. The man was nothing more than a hot smoldering duke.

"What did you say?"

"I said I'm not scared of you." She was pretty sure that's all she had implied. But what had she actually said?

He grabbed her by the waist and hauled her up on his shoulder, and she was pretty sure she heard him mutter, "Hot smoldering duke."

Bah! This was not good.

"Sam, this hauling me around is getting a bit tedious. I *can* walk."

"Fine." He dropped her unceremoniously to the ground and walked to the door. He didn't stop there like she expected, instead, he walked all the way out and didn't come back. Ever.

Well, at least a few minutes must have passed because he

came back carrying a glass. "Drink this."

"No."

"Stop being a child. Drink this so that you sober up."

"Fine." And just to be defiant, she gulped down the drink as fast as she could. Then, to prove she didn't need to be a lady around him (for God knows what reason) she wiped her mouth along her forearm.

But all he said was, "Good. Now let's go."

"Where?"

"I'm taking you to your room and locking you in there."

She stamped her foot.

"Don't be so dramatic, Mimi."

"Don't be such a duke, Sam."

He stepped toward her and her breath shifted direction, causing her to cough.

"I wouldn't have to be the responsible one if you took it up a time or two."

"Hmph!" was her mature reply. And to make it worse, her body chose that moment to yawn. Drat. Of all the times to feel particularly fatigued. "Fine," she said, swaying her arms in whichever direction they felt like going. "Lead the way."

He grunted and walked to the door. This time he waited for her to follow. When he peeked out into the hallway, she stopped behind him. Her hands hovering at his back, not allowing herself to touch him.

"No one's here. Come on." He reached back and grabbed her hand, tugging her out of the library, practically dragging her to her room.

When they arrived in her room, she locked the door behind her out of habit. She felt exhausted, but no longer tipsy. "Can you tell my sister I had a megrim?"

He nodded distractedly.

What made the next words pop out of her mouth, she couldn't be sure because she really couldn't blame the whiskey now. "Help me out of this dress," she said, turning her back to him and waiting.

"What?"

"You want me to sleep this off? I need to sleep. I can't get out of this dress myself. And I can't sleep in this dress."

"Mimi—"

"Just close your eyes, Sam."

She felt him move toward her and she knew she had made a catastrophic mistake. There was no acting indifferent around Sam as he undressed her. She couldn't even feign indifference when he looked at her, never mind when he held her.

But his fingers were already working the buttons. Light brushes of his fingers grazed her (burned her) through her corset. There was no turning back. And no turning around. She had to remind herself of that. Don't twist around in his arms and kiss him. Do not do it. Just breathe. Like a normal person.

"Stop moving," he reprimanded, but his breath was too warm on her neck and she shuddered.

"I'm not moving, I'm breathing."

"Then stop breathing."

She felt his fingers linger and then move on. "There. It's done."

The cool air on her back rushed through her. Without thinking, she turned around and put out her hand requesting his assistance out of her skirts that had pooled at her feet. It was a movement out of habit. One she had done countless times with a lady's maid, but never once with a man. Yet there he was, mouth agape, eyes wide open.

CHAPTER FIFTEEN

HIS EYES HAD turned dark, burrowing into her soul. But instead of recognizing their desire, she said the first thing that came to mind. "I told you to close your eyes."

"I didn't." She thought he should feel some remorse for that decision, but his eyes spoke only of desire.

"I can see that." She stood still, hand out, waiting for his assistance, but he didn't move. "Help me out of this."

Wordlessly, he lifted his hand and acted like the sturdy support she needed to step over the billowing fabric. He was the last man on earth she would have expected support from. Yet somehow it felt like the most natural thing in the world for him to be offering that to her. It was silly to think. It was just his hand. And it was merely holding hers, hardly even holding. One might be better off referring to the touch as a graze. Her body shook as she made her steps. His touch was unnerving. Him in her bedroom was confusing.

She had never had a man in her bedchamber before. Well, since this wasn't even her room, perhaps it still didn't count. So what would it be like to have Sam in her room? Or their room? Him as her husband…that thought was—well, it just had no place here.

"That will be all," she said because she had to say it. She needed to put some distance between them. Class or otherwise.

"I'm not your servant, Mimi." His voice was firm, just like his offered support had been. He was a man who knew who he was. He didn't let other people walk all over him. In fact, he wasn't even the kind to let someone take a single step onto him. But she couldn't stifle her attempts.

She lifted her chin like a queen, "Did you, or did you not just help me out of my dress?"

"I did." The words, like rocks, were ground out of his mouth being pulverized into sand.

"Well then?" It was as silly as any other argument they had had, competing to see who could win a superfluous debate.

"Men often help women out of their clothing."

Bah! Her face flamed. It would seem the point would go to him this round. She had not been expecting that reply, and of course, now all she could think about were husbands all over the world undressing their wives in preparation for…that.

"Just as I thought. You're so naive." He turned toward the door. She should want him to leave. He wasn't supposed to be alone with her, never mind in this room with an oversized bed. Which, now that she looked over to it seemed to be inviting her. Beckoning to her. And she immediately knew that she wanted to stall. He couldn't leave just yet. Not on that note. Not with that tone. Not thinking he had won.

"How dare you say that to me," her tone was demanding, but quiet. There was no need to raise her voice and cause a disturbance.

"Who else would I say it to? You're the only one of my acquaintances acting like a child."

"I'm not acting like a child. I'm a woman."

His eyes dropped to her breasts, and for the first time she considered what he might actually be able to see through her layers. But she didn't let that stop her. In fact, she pushed out her chest to prove her point. Let him stare if he wanted.

"I'm a woman and I can make my own choices. I don't need you interfering in my life."

"Interfering, am I?"

"Yes," she said, but her voice was a bit wobbly.

"So it was your plan all along to snare Roger into a scandal and try to force his hand into marrying you even though he would have refused to do the honorable thing?" Of course he would have to ask that. She wanted to put that event out of her mind, at least in front of Sam, because she still hadn't processed it all. It wasn't clear what had happened. She only knew that part of her—a very tiny part—wanted to defend Roger in front of Sam. She didn't want to look the fool, chasing a man who didn't want her. Not in front of Sam. The last thing she wanted was to appear incompetent in him. He would view that weakness and lord it over her. Or worse, pity her.

First, she wanted him to know that she would never stoop to that level of trapping a man, so she said, "Even if he asked, I wouldn't have accepted the offer. I have my pride."

"Do you? Because the man was refusing to ask."

So she had to defend Roger, as empty as the defense felt even to her own ears. "He wouldn't have refused."

"He did refuse. Didn't you hear him down there?" He was right, but she couldn't let on to that fact. She wasn't done fighting yet, even if she had to spout half-truths. Or full lies.

"Roger is a good man. Unlike you. He would have done the honorable thing." After the words were out, she wasn't sure any of those statements were true, though she wanted to give Roger the benefit of the doubt. And even though now she knew, standing here with Sam, even if Roger had offered, she would have declined.

"You're delusional."

She walked up to him and raised her hand to slap him, but he caught her wrist. Her face was inches from his. "You are an odious man."

"I won't disagree with you."

"You should be punished for how you've been treating me."

Sam's eyes coasted over her body, his intense gaze meeting her eyes. Challenging. Daring.

"*I should be punished?*"

"Yes," her voice actually trembled. She tried to pull her wrist free.

"Me? I'm the one who should be scolded?"

"Yes."

"I don't think so. If anyone needs a spanking, it's you."

A spanking? A tremor wrestled through her muscles. "Wh-why would you say that?"

He licked his bottom lip and his hand gripped her hip. "Because if I spanked you, then you might reconsider your behavior."

Never in all her fantasies had she ever imagined spanking, but the thought of Sam…and his hand…on her bottom…God. Her nipples were pebbling and her body had entered a new climate. Hot and wet. She felt as though she could be wading through a jungle for all the dampness that had suddenly appeared. And wouldn't that be just the fantasy? To be taken on a jungle floor by an astonishingly handsome man that she couldn't stand. Yes. She wanted that to become her reality. Right now. He was offering. In a way. Or she had turned it around so that he thought he thought he had been offering. Either way, this was her chance.

Her bottom lip was tucked into her mouth and her arms were already wrapped around his neck.

"What are you doing?"

"I think you should do it," she whispered in as sultry a voice as she knew how to produce.

"What?" Sam's eyebrows shot to the ceiling.

She inched closer to his mouth, "You should do it. Spank me." She pushed up on her tiptoes and pressed her mouth against his ear. "I dare you."

His voice sounded a bit hoarse, as though his tongue was tangled in one of the large jungle leaves they were currently wading through. "What about Roger?"

"Roger, who?" Roger was…well, confusing. Fate had not dealt her a clear hand. Roger was out.

"So you're not going to pursue your destiny?"

"He's not my destiny." She could say that now because at the very least, she knew that to be true. The man wasn't interested in her. Never had been. She had wasted enough time and effort on him. And now she could see that she had never truly been interested in him. Only in archery and the possibility that fate was speaking to her.

Sam studied her face. "What is your destiny?"

The question was too deep, too personal for the moment. Right now, she didn't care about her destiny. She wanted here and now. She wanted her fantasy. Devil take it, she wanted reality, and reality was a curious thing. Reality was Sam, right in front of her, giving her a good reason to be naughty, and she wanted to take it. He was a gorgeous man. Any woman would gladly take her place, but he was with her. He had chosen her in this moment. He was reprimanding her, but wasn't that some twisted version of protection? He was here for her. That was the point. Was he bluffing when he said he would spank her? She would know soon enough.

"I don't know my destiny. I just want what's here for right now."

He was obviously struggling with making a decision.

"I want a man that knows what he wants, Sam. If you need to think about that or you're not man enou—"

Strands of her hair were flying around her cheeks, she was being hauled—again.

"Don't," he said, tossing her on the bed, "question me, and my manhood."

Breathless, she lay there, waiting for what was about to come.

"Get on your knees."

Oh.

My.

God.

This was happening. She scrambled to her knees, her head hanging between her elbows.

Sam lifted her bottom hem and sucked in his breath.

"I'm going to do this one time and one time only. There are no expectations after this."

"Yes," she mumbled, her heart racing, her arms shaking as they held up her body weight. She wanted his hands on her body. On a part of her that no one had touched. In a way that no one had touched her before. She wanted his scolding. His protection. And she wanted it desperately. She could feel an ache between her legs as she waited. She wanted to peek over her shoulder to see his face, but she could hardly think straight, never mind coordinate the thoughts it would take to turn her head and give him a coy look.

When he spoke, his deep voice reverberated through her stomach and caused her heart to tremble. "This is for almost causing a scandal."

She nodded, but wasn't sure if he could see it—

SMACK!

She groaned. God, if she had been wet earlier, after the ceremony, she was dripping right now. She could feel it seeping down her leg.

Through her groan, she didn't hear what Sam said, but then his hands gripped her waist and she was straddling him. Her core was nestled on either side of a bulge in his breeches, and she moaned at the contact.

She threw her head back, arching her breasts up against him, wanting to feel more.

She needed more, but she had no idea what to do with him. Well...she had some ideas.

CHAPTER SIXTEEN

SAM WAS BEYOND possessed. As Mimi was grinding against his thickening cock he knew he had never been so hard in his life. Her breasts had been thrust before him and he desperately wanted them in his mouth. One hand gruffly glided up her torso and cradled her breast, lifting it to his mouth. He could see where her nipple would be and he was desperate. He let go of her and with two hands wrenched open the layers hiding her breasts.

Her mewl spawned a bottomless desire within him. He needed to hear that sound again, no matter what it took. Taking both of her breasts he pressed them together and sucked one side and then the other into his mouth. Her head was thrown back, lolling slowly from side to side. Her body writhing atop him had evolved from grinding to bouncing lightly, her center pressing and releasing against his throbbing rod.

For a quick contented second, he sat back and watched her breasts dance before him. "God, you're beautiful." The words were out of his mouth before he could put more thought behind them.

"Take me,"—she puffed out the words before adding— "Sam."

His name on her breath. Her hoarse cry. He couldn't deny her. He gripped her hips tightly, following her lead, offering himself up to her for her pleasure. A mixture of groans clouded his thoughts, more so when her hands tunneled through his hair and gripped him hard.

She repeated her earlier plea, and this time he understood it for what it was. A request for guidance, instruction. Perhaps even a request for him to take over her movements. "Sam, take me." It was urgent, her cheek was pressed against his and her mouth was against his ear this time. He could feel her heartbeat pulsating through her chest.

There was nothing he liked more than being in control in the bedroom, but there was something about Mimi he wanted to know in a different way. He would normally give in to her request in a trice, but this time he wanted her to lead this experience. He wanted to see what she wanted. What she liked. What she would do. How she would find her pleasure using him.

"No, Mimi. You do it. Take me and find your pleasure." And the words were like the splitting of a dam. Her hips ground into his. Her hands were all over his body, capturing the muscles in his stomach. Pressing into his chest. Kneading his shoulders. Cupping his jaw. Holding the back of his head like she would never let go. He had been held by countless women in his life, many experienced women, but this was different. This was passion and connection. An intimacy he had never felt before.

"There…ah…yes, Sam." Her words were stilted, but her movements were fluid. He could feel the tightening in his lower back. The heaviness in his sack. The base of his cock solid as steel. There was no skin to skin contact apart from their face and hands, yet still he was the most aroused he had ever been. "Yes…uh…uh…yes, yes." Just before she screamed his name, his hand flew up to cover her mouth and muffle the cry that would surely ruin her, "Sam!"

The spasm in her body threw him over the edge. His legs went numb, his cock was like granite, and hot liquid gushed out of him into his breeches. He hadn't done that…possibly ever. His cock twitched as she squeezed once last ounce of pleasure from him. Warmed in the fluid, his rod had never felt such satisfaction.

Slumped against his body, her head rested against his shoulder. After taking a few minutes to steady his breathing and regain strength in his legs, he swept her in his arms and stood. She was barely awake, so he laid her in her bed, brushed her hair from her forehead, and kissed her temple, tucking her in for the night.

IT WAS THE afternoon of the archery tournament, the most exciting part of this whole house party. Save for last night with Mimi. Oh, and the wedding. The reason they had all gathered. Of course, Sam should have a vested interest in the wedding…and he did. Sort of. Jacob was a friend. Sally was a nice lady. The two were in love. And so on and so forth. Greatest day of their lives. Yes. That's what they believed. Sam wasn't convinced. Yes, he believed they were in love. But he knew only too well what an all-consuming love like theirs could lead to. So, back to the point, he was more keen on the archery tournament than the wedding at this point.

And really, calling it a tournament was a bit of a stretch. It was an activity that had been postponed and now the competitive few had had too much time to build up the event in their minds. There was no prize for the winner except the knowledge that they had beat a few other archers.

Waiting for the event to begin, Sam took up a place near the barrel. The same one upon which he had arm wrestled Mimi. Had he really called her a child so recently? Even when he had addressed her as such, he hadn't really thought of her as a child. She was a woman, but he had needed the distance between them. Something about her was too electrifying to go near. And now he knew firsthand exactly how electrifying she was. Her passion. Her willingness. Her desire. It stoked a fire in him that he needed to quell. Yet there was no part of him that desired a future being married.

Lost in his thoughts, it took Mimi's squeal (of all things) to bring him back to the present. Sally and Jacob were walking toward everyone with arms full of arrows.

"A special gift for our guests," Sally announced while Jacob grinned next to her. They placed the gifts directly in front of Sam and a few hands were quick to reach in and grab their favorite pieces. When he reached his hand in to snag an arrow that caught his eye, his fingers brushed against another hand. Without looking up, he knew it was Mimi. A spark had fluttered between them.

When his eyes met hers, a flicker of uncertainty flashed in her eyes. They hadn't spoken since last night. He had nothing to say to her. Well, that wasn't true. He just didn't know what the appropriate thing to say was to a virgin he had slightly debauched the night before. He had told her there were no expectations, and as far as he could interpret her body language, she didn't hold anything against him. Only…he wasn't sure if he wished she would or not.

"Is that what you like?" he asked her.

Her eyes darkened, and he knew she was envisioning the night before. That smallest of gestures of desire sent a pulse through to his cock. But this was neither the time nor the place.

"Do you want it?" Her bewilderment gave him reason to further the question. "The arrow…is that the one you want?" They were both still holding onto the arrow, his pinky slightly grazing over her thumb.

When she nodded, he lifted the arrow out of the basket. Her brows furrowed and it seemed almost as though she blinked back a look of loss.

"It's yours." He handed her the arrow.

"Really?"

"Of course. You think I would take it for myself knowing that you want it?"

"I–I–"

And he had his answer. An answer to a question he didn't even realize he had been asking. She really did think the worst of him. For her to think he would be so selfish as to take an object of her affection for himself…he willed himself to hide his effrontery.

"Thank you."

"No thanks is required. Really." He turned and walked away. Now all he wanted to do was get this bloody tournament over with, despite his eagerness earlier to participate.

"Archers, take your places," Sally called out.

Sam took a second to look around and his eye caught sight of James. A rare sighting indeed. The man must have just shown up. This should be fun.

Chris walked over, taking his place next to Sam. "Are we betting on this?"

"Of course we are."

Chris laughed. "What's your bet?"

"Mimi for five hundred pounds."

At the name and number, Chris coughed. "Really?"

"Yes."

"And you're not going to throw it?"

Another insult. Sam could feel his insides churning as though the cook was making butter in there. He threw Chris a look. "Do you honestly think I would ever do such a thing?"

Chris shrugged. "For the right woman."

"Ha! I would never do that." He struck his finger through the air, oddly mimicking the theatrics of a particularly outspoken and irritating blonde woman he knew. "Do you even know me?" He had no plans whatsoever in throwing the tournament, but he had witnessed Mimi's abilities, and if he had to bet on anyone, it would be her. Obviously the thought crossed his mind that he should place the wager on himself…but for some reason it didn't feel right. And hadn't he told Mimi that he only bet knowing he would win? Well, then…Mimi was the right bet.

Chris shook his head just before the next calls were made.

As they all stood at the ready, Sam took a glance down the line to take note of both Roger and Mimi. He could see the determination in her face. Her body was pulled tight as if it were stressed, but he could sense the calmness in her. She was…inspiring.

Sam released her from his gaze and exhaled, focusing on the target in front of him. She was a worthy opponent, and he wanted to beat her. That sounded terrible, didn't it? A man wanting to beat a woman at a game that didn't matter. Yet he knew she was a competitor. In her heart, she was fierce. She would always compete at her best, and she would expect that out of others. At least those that she respected. She wouldn't respect him if he didn't do his best. And somehow, her good opinion of him, her respect for him mattered a great deal.

"Ready…aim…fire!"

Arrows soared. His was a bullseye, or appeared to be. He looked down the line and caught Mimi's grin. Then his eyes shot back down to the targets to see where her arrow landed. He thought his arrow had hit dead center, but he could see now that he was wrong.

James's and Roger's arrows were close, his closer, but Mimi's…yes, Sally was confirming it. This round went to Mimi.

Round two had all the archers quiet. They could see the competition for what it was now, and they all grew just a bit more eager to win.

The second arrows all flew a touch faster than the previous round, and each archer's aim improved. Mimi struck dead center again. The small audience of house guests was murmuring now. Perhaps debunking any suggestions that Mimi's first shot had been coincidence or luck.

Mimi and Sam both scored a point in the second round. She nodded graciously to him, and he returned one in kind.

It was the last round, there was only a chance that he could even the scores, so the other archers dropped out.

The final flight soared through the air as though floating. Light but intentional.

When his eyes finally focused on his target, he saw his arrow was slightly off center. But he didn't need to see that to acknowledge his loss. The cheers around Mimi were instantane-ous, boisterous, and joyous. They were celebrating her success, and she deserved it.

He couldn't help the piercing jealousy that invaded his body. Not because she won though. James had run up to her and was swinging her around in the air. Sam chuffed a laugh. They were about to be family, but really, that seemed a bit much. If anyone should be swinging her in the air, it should be him. Sam.

But he couldn't do it. That expressiveness. That kind of im-pulsive behavior around women only led to destruction.

CHAPTER SEVENTEEN

"CONGRATULATIONS, MIMI." SAM'S words shifted through her, unsettling in her stomach. Her hands gripped her silly little trophy as she stood before him balancing on her toes and then rocking back on her heels. The cheers had died down and the small crowd had dispersed. They had already taken off to the next activity of the day.

He said he would be happy for her if she beat him in something, and sure enough, the man had a smile on his face. Perhaps a bit tight around the eyes, but he was genuine. She could read him. Somehow the past few days had taught her more about the man than she realized.

He was happy for her. Celebrating her. So why was she disappointed? What did she expect? For *him* to be the one to swing her up and around in his arms? She knew who he was, and that wasn't him. That wasn't his style...and really, she did know him. He didn't want to invest. He didn't want a future with someone. Why would he let his emotions out of their dark den if he didn't want the light of a future with her? Did she even want one with him? Of course she did. Who was she trying to deceive?

The duke dare be damned...or actualized...she wanted him. And she would do whatever it took to get him.

"Are you proud of yourself?" Sam was speaking again, filling the silence that she had left unintentionally.

"Yes, thank you," she answered demurely. When did she ever

act timidly like this? But she felt unsure of herself. Or…more accurately, she felt unsure of herself around him now. Only because she knew the effect he had on her. She knew the effect she wanted him to have on her. What she didn't know, was how to get him to want the same thing.

"No thanks necessary."

"Well, you did let me have the arrow."

"Any gentleman would do the same thing."

"Not everyone." She wanted to tell him the quiver story; it was on the tip of her tongue, but something was holding her back. She steadied her eyes on him, not permitting herself to break the contact. And as she stared, a realization dawned on him.

"The quiver?" His eyes were curious and held some disbelief, so she only nodded. "Your destiny?"

"We both know that nothing about that incident was my destiny, especially not the navy-and-gold quiver."

She watched as his eyes flickered with recollection. He might have noticed Roger's quiver. It was the only one of its kind that she had seen before, but she didn't want to dwell on it.

"I should go—"

"I bet on you," he interrupted her lackluster attempt to flee.

The phrase came from the skies, clear out of nowhere, befuddling her. "Wh-hat? What do you mean?"

"I thought you would win." His smile was huge now, covering his entire face, pushing his cheeks back and out of the way.

"Wait. Did you bet on me knowing you would throw the competition? You wouldn't, would you?" She felt foolish even asking, but she had to know.

The narrowing of his eyes, in frustration and…hurt…was her answer. But instead of lashing out at her, he shook his head. "No. No, I didn't do that. I would never do that. You should know that by now." And he said it as though they shared a secret. That he knew her and she knew him, and they each appreciated the depth of that knowledge.

The lump in her throat only increased when he added, "I believe in you."

Those words hurt. Not in an insulting way, of course not. In a way that spoke to her soul. In a way that she wanted to close off to him until she knew for certain what his intentions were. If he was an arrogant cad and treated her gruffly, it was easy to hold her emotions at bay. But if he acted like this...celebrating her, seeing her, believing in her. Betting on *her*...then, it was much harder to forget how he held her and how right that had felt.

It was too much. So despite being the one to always raise hell, confront anyone at anytime about anything, she said words she didn't mean and had never intended to use. "I have to go."

"Wait—"

But she had already turned on her heel and raced off. There was no destination except away from him. It was stupid. She knew she was a fool. Falling for a rake. Falling for a man who could never love her. A man who didn't believe in marriage. But knowing she was a fool couldn't stop her from being a fool. Her only saving grace was that she wouldn't be caught playing the fool in front of him. Now she knew her heart. She would stay away from him until this blasted house party was over. Then she would avoid him forever.

Well, apparently avoiding him forever would not start now. She could hear his footsteps thudding lightly behind her. Why he would choose now to chase after her, was beyond her ability to process in the moment. She only tried to run faster. It was no use. She had hardly reached the garden, hidden by the rose trellis, when he caught up to her.

His hand wrapped around her upper arm. Firm, but kind.

"Mimi, what are you doing?"

"I'm running. I thought that was clear." It was mortifying that she was panting heavily, and he was hardly affected by the jog.

He chuckled softly. "Yes, I suppose that is the obvious answer. May I inquire as to why you're running?"

"Why are you being so nice to me right now?"

"What?"

"Sam, what are *you* doing? That is the better question."

"What are you talking about?" When he stepped back a half step, his hand was still upon her. Only it had trailed down her arm and was now clasped around her wrist.

"I mean, why are you chasing me?"

"I-I just followed after you to see if you were all right."

"I'm fine." But from the way she shouted the words at him, she accepted that they could both interpret the equivocation.

"You're not fine. Tell me what's wrong."

"You can't fix it." Only…he could fix it. He was, in fact, the only one who could fix it, but she couldn't tell him that. She thought herself nearly fearless, but facing unrequited love had to be the most terrifying thing she could imagine. And she couldn't bring herself to face it at this moment. She wanted the win of the tournament in her mind, not the inevitable loss (if one could call it losing if one never had it) of love.

She could feel a sting behind her eyes. Dratted tears. She would not drop a tear in front of him. She would not.

His thumb pressed gently over her cheek wiping away a stray raindrop. It had to be from the skies, for surely it had not fallen from her eyes.

She was a giant bundle of nerves. Like tangled yarn. There was no separating the string. It was a mess that would take far too long to unravel. And even though she didn't want to, she looked up into his eyes, desperate to see what consolation he could provide. His thumb on her cheek was not enough. His eyes were dark, his lids drooped down, and his chin tilted. He was leaning in…closer.

Where once his thumb had swept her tear, now his lips pressed the moisture deeper into her cheeks. When he lifted his mouth, her eyes were closed, but she could feel the tear being wicked away. Stolen.

This was the comfort she craved. And it was coming from a man she knew but couldn't put her hope into.

For a brief moment she allowed herself to feel lost in that first kiss and then second kiss on her cheek that was drying her tears. The tears that she didn't want to fall but had fallen all because of her heart that was still falling. There was no ground beneath her. Everything was tumbling down around her. The only thing holding her up was Sam, one hand on her waist, one hand cupping her jaw, and his lips against her cheek.

This moment, here, in his arms, felt right. Like it could be so much more than what they had already shared. He was protective, caring, compassionate, and competitive. He knew what he wanted and he went for it. Why couldn't he want her?

A tainted thought slipped through the cracks of her ethics. She could trap him. She could make him hers. If they were caught alone together, he would have to do the honorable thing—the same thing he had demanded of Roger—and marry her.

It was too easy. She could sneak away and set it up so that a small group of people would find them, and then he would marry her. She would have him…but even as she planned it out, she knew she wouldn't have him. Not all of him anyway. She might have his name, his hand, a ring, his status…that was all. And it wasn't worth it. She couldn't trap him, intentionally or accidentally.

"I can't be here," she whispered. His lips grazed her jaw.

"Why not?"

"We could be caught at any moment."

The slight stiffening of his body told her everything she needed to know. She had said the right thing, and now she needed to do the right thing. She needed to move her feet and leave—

"What's going on here?" a voice boomed, splitting them apart.

Mimi gasped, looking up. Several pairs of eyes were staring back at her, stunned. It wasn't just one person, or even a couple of people (ideally her sisters), no, it was everyone. Or at least enough of everyone to matter.

James and Joan. Sally and Jacob. Roger. Chris and Nobi. Sally's parents. Where had they been this whole time? Of course they showed up now. Had the succeeding activity to archery been an investigative walk? This was the worst possible situation Mimi could have found herself in.

If it had only been Roger who discovered them, he probably wouldn't have batted an eye, considering his dismissal of honor. If it had been her sisters, they would have been convinced to keep it mum. But *everyone*? There was not a chance in all of England that she would get away from this scenario without a forced proposal.

In a similar situation, Joan had been strong enough, independent enough, resilient enough to refuse to be pushed around by societal expectations. But Mimi was desperate. Her heart was already owned by Sam, and she knew she wanted him. If this was the way to get him, she wasn't going to be a fool. She was going to take it. Even if she had to work that much harder to make him fall for her after marriage, she'd do it.

Sam cleared his throat. "I was just stealing a moment with…my betrothed." If he hadn't choked out the last two words, she might have been able to lie to herself about his feelings on the matter. But the look in his eye, the one which spoke of terror and dread, yes…that look was most unbecoming on a fiancé.

He stepped closer to her, back into her space. But it no longer felt comforting, it felt constrained. Was this really what she wanted? His arm snaked around her back, and she could relate to Adam and Eve wanting to hide in the garden. She felt exposed, and the snake at her back was not the ally she wished him to be.

This was her moment though. By his presence alone, she could feel him prodding her to say something.

She should release him from the obligation. She could be like Joan. She could be a strong, independent woman, braced, prepared, and equipped to manage her own mistakes. She should exonerate him from this ludicrous situation. She should be strong enough *for herself* to take care of herself and her future. She didn't need anyone. She should be strong enough, damn it.

And she was…

But she also knew what she wanted. And she felt the fool—or not fool—acting up in her. "Yes, just a quick moment alone was all we required."

After the first few, Mimi stopped counting the raised brows, never mind the slack jaws. Apparently no one would have bet on the two of them getting more acquainted. But then Mimi caught a gleam in Nobi's eyes…perhaps her sister saw something. She would have to speak with her later. For now, the emotions roiling through her were practically throwing her off balance. Regrettably, she leaned into Sam's shoulder for support. His arm pulled her in closer.

"Well, I never—" someone started to say, but Mimi couldn't make out who.

"Shall we have tea as planned and let the couple have their moment?" Ever supportive of her, Joan was indirectly instructing the group. "I shall remain as a chaperone with James." Heads nodded and bodies turned. A few looked back to confirm that indeed they had witnessed what they were in obvious disbelief over: Sam and Mimi.

After everyone had left, besides family, Mimi blinked up at her sisters, quelling her tears. Twice in a few moments just would not do.

"Are you all right?" Nobi was at her side in a flash, her hand on Mimi's forearm. Mimi only nodded her response.

"Take your moment, Mimi. We'll be just over there." Joan pointed to the other side of the roses. "We can discuss this afterward. This may be a scandal, but it's nothing we can't handle together. We will stand behind you no matter what you decide." And she had this knowing look in her eyes as she voiced her support. As if she knew it was different between Mimi and Sam.

She watched her sisters walk away. Boudicca had Wes, Joan was about to have James, and Nobi would have Chris (surely, that would happen). They would have all married for love. And then there would be Mimi. Alone. Married by scandal. Rescued from ruin. She couldn't save herself…not the way she wanted to. Her future had never before looked so empty. It made her furious to feel so constricted. Imprisoned. This marriage would shackle her just as much, if not more so than Sam. But she would have him…

Her heart pounded through her ears. This was everything she wanted wrapped up in everything that she didn't want.

To hell with it all, there was only one way forward. Without even looking at Sam, she announced, "You're marrying me, whether you like it or not." And she stomped off.

Chapter Eighteen

I T WASN'T ENOUGH, but it had to be. He knew he couldn't give her what she wanted, what she deserved. She was a woman with a dreamer's heart. She wanted love. She wanted the fantasy. He couldn't give it to her, and he planned to tell her that. As a caution...a reminder...a way to set the expectation for their marriage. But he needed a buffer. He couldn't simply visit her before their wedding and disclose his lack of love for her. And it had nothing to do with the inkling of a feeling that he wanted to go through with the wedding.

It was just a quiver. Again, not enough to make up for an empty ocean of feelings, but perhaps just enough to show that he cared. Because...well, he did care about her. He obviously couldn't deny that he wanted to protect her. He just...well, he really could not allow himself to obsess over her.

Those were the reasons he stood in front of her door the night before the wedding and knocked quietly. He heard a soft shuffling and then the door creaked open slightly.

"Sam?"

"Let me in. I have something for you," he whispered, squeezing his broad shoulders through the narrow slit she had left open.

"It's after midnight," she said sleepily, wiping her eyes.

He huffed. "I didn't think it would take me as long as it did, but I had to do it."

"The special license?" she asked.

"Yes, among other things I had to do."

"Do what?" He watched as she stifled a yawn.

"Were you sleeping?" It was a stupid question, but one he couldn't take back. She just yawned in response. "I'm sorry. This can wait." What had possessed him to gift the present now? He could have waited until morning...but here he was, practically holding her up with his eyes she was so tired.

"I'm up now. What is it?" She plopped herself down in an armchair, palms up on her thighs.

"This is for you." He handed over the package. "It's a wedding present."

"Oh, I didn't get you anything—"

"No, you weren't meant to. I just,"—he raked his hands through his hair—"know this is difficult for you."

"For me?"

And he knew he needed to start their marriage, however flimsy it would be, with truth. "You want the dream, Mimi."

Her cocked brow prodded him to continue.

"You want the fantasy. The love. All of it. But scandal has forced your hand."

His words must have probed something inside of her, for she sat upright now. "I'm not being forced to do anything. If I didn't want to do it, I wouldn't."

Of course she would put on a brave face. She was fearless. Mostly.

"I understand—"

"Actually, I don't think you do. I have my reasons to marry you. And it's not just because of the scandal." Her arms were crossed over her chest now. Her signature gesture of stubbornness.

"What are your reasons?" And he shouldn't do it, but he had to ask, "Do you...have feelings for me?" It was rude, selfish, and arrogant to ask the question. Especially when he knew (didn't he?) his answer.

She studied him for a beat and then replied. "You're a duke.

You're kind. You're close with two of my sisters' husbands, or soon-to-be. We shall all be quite close. It will be lovely."

But the tone impressed upon the word lovely didn't quite ring as prettily as it should have. It sounded like the way a woman said everything would be fine even though everything was chaos and *fine* was not on the horizon. But he wanted to give her the benefit of the doubt.

Her hands twitched against the wrapping of the gift in her lap. "Are you going to open it?" he asked. It was as good a time as any to change the conversation. It wasn't fair to press her about her feelings.

Without even looking up, she murmured, "Yes, thank you." And her hands were tearing away the paper.

She didn't say a word as he observed her pulling out a navy-blue-and-gold quiver. Her hands ran down the sides and along the embellishments. Though her hands revealed reverence, her lips were pulled down at the corners.

"Do you like it?" He had to know.

"Yes," she answered in a hush tone. "It's perfect." It was all she said as she stared at the quiver.

And he couldn't help wondering if it was a good thing or not to enter their friends' wedding day with perfection. In one way it was good. A clean slate (of sorts), a kind and considerate beginning. Then again, it could all be downhill from here on out. Her facial expression was impossible to read.

"We should sleep." When he stood up and offered his hand, she gave him a look of surprise and shot a quick glance at her bed.

"Uh…I'll be going to my room. You sleep here."

Her eyes narrowed at him. "Of course that's how it will be." She jumped to her feet without taking his hand, clearly wide awake in irritation now.

"I'll see you tomorrow," he said. And before either of them could change their mind, he leaned forward and pressed a light kiss to her temple. "Sleep well."

MIMI STOOD NEXT to Sally readying herself to go down the aisle. Her quiver from Sam slung over her shoulder, resting against her back. It felt right.

The ceremonies were going to happen together. Joan had already been by to express her shock that Mimi was getting married before her, but she was only delighted for her sister. They had all shared an embrace, and now Joan and Nobi were in the sanctuary waiting for her entrance. A twinge of guilt infused itself in her conscience. She should be happy, if not as overjoyed as Sally, then at least not as mopey as she felt.

Sam's gift last night was more confusing than anything, but she didn't want to burden anyone with her complaints. She knew how shallow they would sound. *Poor me, marrying a duke. A handsome man with a good heart. Only, he hasn't said he loves me.* It sounded awfully ridiculous to her own ears, so she hadn't yet voiced her thoughts to anyone.

The music started. It was their cue to start walking down, first Sally and then Mimi. But Sally didn't budge.

"What's wrong?" Mimi immediately put her worries aside to consider her friend.

Sally turned to face her. "It's not me. It's you."

"Oh God, I'm sorry Sally. I didn't mean to take over your wedding. Sam and I can marry on a different day."

Sally reached out her hand, placing it on Mimi's wrist. "It's not that. It's just...you don't look happy."

The music was playing, the people were waiting. It was Sally's day. She had been looking forward to it for a while now, yet here she was checking in on Mimi's feelings.

"You're a good friend, Sally."

"So are you. I wouldn't be with Jacob if it weren't for you and your sisters."

That was true, Mimi wasn't even sure if she knew the extent

of effort each sister had put forth to ensure Sally and Jacob's union.

"I can't walk down this aisle with you in this state." Her grip tightened. "I want you to be as happy as I am. I wish I could make it so." A shimmer caught Mimi's eye.

"You have a wonderful heart, Sally. I just don't know if I can share in that depth of emotion considering the reason I'm getting married."

"What reason is that?" Either Sally was feigning ignorance to the obvious incident that caused this budding nuptial, or she had somehow forgotten.

"The scandal."

"You think you're marrying Sam because of the scandal?"

"Of course."

Sally let Mimi's words cloud the air as she hummed out her consideration of them.

When she said nothing, Mimi prodded her, "You don't agree?"

"I don't know, Mimi. I never really considered you the type to just marry a man because society might try to shun you if you didn't."

"Well…"

"Are you really trying to tell me that you have no other justification in marrying him other than the scandal?"

"Well…" she repeated the profound phrase.

"And are you trying to convince me or yourself that Sam, the self-proclaimed bachelor for eternity, offered to protect you only because of this scandal?"

"Um…"

Sally clucked her tongue. "Really, Mimi. You must open your eyes."

"It's just that…yes, I like him." Oh, it was more than like at this point, but she didn't want to admit that aloud. "But he doesn't…love me."

More silence ensued, threatening to break Mimi's sanity, or at least her resolve to await Sally's reply.

"I saw the way he looked at you when you walked down the aisle to him."

Heat rushed her face. A ribbon of hope swirled through her stomach, catching up with her heart, and pulling it taut. She had felt something that day too but didn't want to admit it.

"H-how did he look at me?"

"I shouldn't be the one to tell you," Sally said.

"Who should?"

"He'll tell you. In time. In his own way."

Ugh. Mimi groaned which made Sally chuckle.

"I know that's not what you wanted to hear. But you need to trust him."

"How do you trust someone you don't know?"

Sally chuckled again. "It's funny that you should think that. You do know him. Trust yourself and trust him, Mimi." She turned to go but hesitated and turned back. "I should like to add one more thing. I'm sorry your mother isn't here," she reached in for a quick embrace. "She would be so proud of you. So I just want to say that my mother spoke with me last night—"

"Oh, please don't tell me about the bedroom—"

Laughter peeled out of Sally. "I wouldn't dare. But my mother did give me some sage advice. Marriage is the hardest thing you will ever choose to do in your life because it's not just one choice. It's a million little choices every day. And then you have to make the same choices again the next day and the next. Every day you have to choose love. Not fear. You have to choose to trust your husband. Give him the benefit of the doubt. And, the hardest part of all, give all of yourself to him. That's assuming you want all of him in return. And I think you do." Her voice quieted at the last few words. "You two are going to be very happy together. I can feel it. Just let yourself love him. Choose love."

And even though Mimi didn't say the words aloud to her friend, hearing Sally say them sunk into her soul. "Thank you,

Sally." She blinked hard to hold back the tears. "Now let's walk down this aisle and get married."

The ceremony was over in a blur with the only moments of clarity being when Sam said, *I do*, and then later when he had kissed her in front of everyone. His eyes were sincere, if nothing else. They were full of emotion that she couldn't read, mostly because her own feelings were overwhelming.

By the time the reception started, Mimi felt as though the blurriness had cleared and she could finally process the smaller details that were right in front of her. She was married. All right, that wasn't a small detail. Rather large in the grand scheme of life. Sam, her husband, was sharing a drink with a group of friends, and Mimi was taking it all in and her sisters were soon at her side.

"I can't believe you're married," Joan said, shaking her head. "First the eldest, then the youngest."

"It wasn't planned that way," Mimi answered. "I'm still in shock myself. But...it's all going to work out."

"Of course it will. This is you, Mimi. This is your life. You will make the best of it," Nobi's arm was around her waist, holding her in a side embrace. "You wouldn't let a little thing like marriage change you." She nudged her. "Besides, this isn't the worst possible outcome. I'd rather say it's much closer to the perfect possible outcome, wouldn't you agree?"

Mimi eyed her sister. "You think this is the best possible outcome?"

"Close to it. If you're willing to admit it," Nobi batted back.

But Mimi only shrugged.

"I overheard Sam say that you'll be heading back to his estate tonight."

That was news to her, but she supposed it made sense. Their first night as husband and wife should be together in his house.

"That means there's only a few hours left here." And there was a trace of melancholy in that statement.

"We had better make the most of it," Joan added cheerily.

"We'll all be together shortly for your wedding, Joan," Nobi reminded them.

"True! And Boudicca will be back by then, so it will really be all of us."

"In the meantime, let's dance."

The reception was taking place outside under large tents. Food and drinks abounded, and already a few guests were three or four sheets to the wind. The music was vibrant and enticing, so Mimi let herself be pulled into the effervescence of the event.

Mimi had danced with a few gentlemen and was taking a short break to have a drink when Sam finally broke free from the group he had been talking to and walked over to her.

"May I have this dance, wife?" he asked with a gleam in his eye.

"Of course," she answered and curtsied.

Placing her hand in his, she felt the tingle she always felt with him and wondered if he sensed it too. Realizing now that those sensations were unique to him, and she wouldn't feel that with any man, she allowed her heart a moment of hope. As they took their place in the dance, they could hear the light patter of rain against the tent. There was a slight chill in the air, but nothing too cold. The dance began and Mimi was pleased to know it was a waltz. Their first dance together *should be* a waltz. She was lost in the feel of his hands on her body and gracefully floating through the steps when a commotion in the middle of the tent put pause to their steps.

Someone was drunk. It looked innocent enough until the man said something he obviously shouldn't have and then the first punch was thrown. Men were clamoring to pull apart the two rivals, but in all the chaos the mass of men was thrown into the center pole holding up the tent.

Down. Down. Down went the town.

Rain sluiced down the fabric soaking everything in its path. Still in Sam's arms, Mimi was instantly soaked.

"God, I'm sorry, Mimi, let's get you inside and dry."

This was a disaster. Or…

"No," she said, smiling up at him. "Let's just dance."

— ❧ ❧ ❧ —

CHAPTER NINETEEN

S TANDING IN FRONT of the mirror, Mimi stood awaiting Sam's return to his bedchamber. Yes, his bedchamber in his house. After the dance, they had dried off and she had been whisked away to her new home. By the time they arrived home, it was too dark for introductions of any kind. And Sam had left her in his room to get ready while he went away and did…well, she had no idea what he was doing.

And she had no idea what he was expecting.

It was their wedding night. She knew what was supposed to happen, and she knew what she wanted. Him.

This was her chance. Her choice. To remain brave in the face of real fear, in the face of rejection. She would offer herself to him, fully, and she could only hope that he would offer in return as much as he could. She would choose love.

She was wearing a translucent negligee that had been secretly packed in her trousseau by one of the women in her life who knew what was needed for the night.

A light tap on the door startled her, bringing her arms around her waist. But that wasn't where she wanted them. She wanted to portray her confidence, so she steeled her hands on her hips, nerves wrought with vibrating steel, as if someone had banged her with a hammer and left the reverberations to simmer through her.

"Mimi, are you—" Sam stopped mid-sentence, catching sight

of her. Visibly, she watched as the air was sucked from his lungs. His eyes climbing her body from toe to head, ambling back down, and slowly, deliberately, crawling up again. The only thing holding her up was an invisible cord through her spine attached to the ceiling. She felt like a puppet, and somehow Sam was the marionette, controlling her from afar.

"You look…" His voice caught again as he stepped closer. His hands stroked her arm and she closed her eyes. "I didn't expect this. I didn't expect you to—"

But she didn't want him to finish his thoughts. She didn't want to know. She just wanted him. Her eyes flew up and she rushed up on her toes, pressing her lips against his.

He was as surprised as she was, and he held her jaw in his hand to speak.

"Mimi, I—"

"I want this, Sam. I want you. You're my husband. Show me what only a husband can do. Show me how a husband treats his wife."

With a growl he picked her up. "You're damn right I'm your husband. And I'll show you what no other man can. What no other man ever will. You're mine."

It wasn't a vow of undying love, but they were the words she needed in order to feel right about giving herself to him. If she offered herself up to him and he didn't accept her gift, that would have devastated her, but here he was, ready, willing, able, and determined to make her his.

His lips were on the column of her neck, and she could feel her breasts rubbing against the single layer of unbuttoned linen that covered his chest.

His familiar scent of tea and whiskey, mixed with sandalwood permeated her body with something soothing yet wild. She wanted her body closer to him, to rub against every muscle of his, to feel his power and control.

His hands were on her bottom, squeezing and lightly kneading into her. Opening her up. She could feel the muscles moving within her that she didn't even know existed. Remembering his passion and the way her body reacted to him, she let go of any outside thoughts. There were no worries in his arms, no external problems to consider. No one to help. Only herself.

His lips were on her nipple, soaking through the light gauzy fabric. He hummed his appreciation of her turgid peaks and a swell of pleasure rolled through her. Shoving her hands under his shirt, she clawed at his shoulders, grazing her nails atop his skin.

He groaned his pleasure and thrust his hips up into her. She could feel the bulge in his breeches and wanted to rub against him. Over and over.

"I'm taking you to my bed now where I'll do whatever I want with you."

Yes. Yes. Yes. This was her fantasy. This was her dream. This was her reality.

Her lips found his as he brought them closer to the bed. After dropping her onto the bed, she whimpered her delight, and he pressed his body down upon her.

"Is this what you like? You want me to take you?"

"Take what's yours," she whispered, hardly managing the words.

His elbows braced her sides. "I will take what's mine." His teeth sunk into her neck, and she arched her back, forcing her nipples to cut into his rippling chest. His shirt was torn from his body and he sat up, untying and then peeling off her negligee.

His eyes grazed her body again, this time seeing her fully. "God, you're the most stunning woman I've ever seen, Mimi."

She didn't allow herself time to reflect on those words, but stored them in her heart to cherish always. Instead, she reached up and pulled him closer to her, desperate for his heat. Urgently needing his lips upon her, and her hands roaming his body.

She caressed his neck and gripped tightly onto his biceps. She could feel him flexing his muscles beneath her grasp, the gesture pooled heat between her thighs.

His head dipped down her body and her stomach hollowed

out. She could feel his breath on her most private parts.

"Sam?" It was a quaking plea. She felt crazed, needing, urgently, but unsure what he was—

"Oooooooh…" A moan flashed out of her lips. His tongue was licking her.

"You taste so sweet, Mimi."

Her hands plunged into his hair, holding him in place. She never knew she would need this sensation, his tongue on her essence. He was feasting on her, devouring her, yet tenderly.

When his tongue stopped, she whimpered. But the beat lasted only a second before he was sucking on her pearl. And God, she didn't want this ever to end.

Calling his name, she could feel herself tensing, but in the best conceivable way. His stubble burned brilliantly against her groin, and she moaned again. And then, as he continued to suck on her, he reached up and gently squeezed her nipple. A flash of white tore through her like lightning in the darkest sky. Pleasure rippled through her like thunder, and the rains of pleasure flooded her.

When he looked up at her, half-lidded, he said, "That's my girl. Now you're ready for me."

Oh.

My.

God.

What had she gotten herself into? There was more? Her limbs were weak, but if there were more, she wanted it. She wanted it all.

"Yes," she murmured. "I want you."

He stood and dropped his breeches, and she watched as his cock bobbed out. He was thick and hard. And God, was he large. If she had her full senses about her, she might be convincing herself that he wouldn't fit inside of her, but all she heard were his reassuring words. *Now you're ready for me.*

Mimi regarded Sam's manhood. What she had thought about the quiver could only truly be said about what she saw before her. *This* was the most incredible, singular piece of equipment she had ever seen.

So she rested on the bed while he placed himself at her entrance. He brushed his cock down her slit, pulling and pushing moisture at his will. She was so tender that each touch compelled her to moan.

"Open for me, Mimi," he leaned over her body and whispered the words into her ear. The soft breath tickled her body all the way down her ribcage, and her legs fell apart further, widening for him.

His tip pressed against her, and it was the most captivating sensation she had ever felt. She was made for him, and as he pressed in, inch by glorious inch, she was only more and more convinced of that fact.

Her body wrapped itself around him, clenching him, as if to never let him go.

"God, you're so tight, Mimi. You're choking me." His voice was ragged in her ear, but each time he spoke, she felt wetter.

"Tell me more," she groaned.

"Mmm…" he moaned against her cheek. "So hot. So wet. For me. Take me in, Mimi."

And now she knew that as much as she wanted him to take her, her body, as a woman, was meant to receive, and she wanted to take him into herself.

He grunted at the movement, found his breath again, and then thrust into her.

"Uhh…" she called out, at a loss for words. The pleasure was rampant inside of her. Around her. Encompassing only them.

"Come for me, Mimi. Again." He called for her, commanded her, and her body responded. She could feel the base of his cock rubbing her pearl, pushing, pulling, teasing, giving. Relentlessly.

The intermingling of them screaming each other's names wrenched the air, as release poured through them.

"Thank God, you're my wife." Sam's last words embedded themselves in her brain as they collapsed in slumber.

WHEN IT RAINED, it poured. Sam knew it to be true, and he was floundering. He was falling for Mimi. But he couldn't be. He needed to keep his wits about him. He would not—would not—turn into his father. He would not be the kind to be so desperately in love with a woman that he was not in control of his own emotions and actions.

Yet…last night was shaping up to be an exception. Forget shaping up, last night was a pointed example of an exception. He had lost himself in her. The moment he saw her he knew he was gone.

He had to set some boundaries. And that was the plan this morning. And God, there were a few boundaries that needed to be set. He hoped that he could do so without too much trouble from his cousin, Rudolph. They had arrived so late last night that there had been no time for introductions. He only hoped that he could send Rudolph on his way without incident. If only he should be so lucky.

Sam sat at the breakfast table awaiting his wife as he planned how to manage Mimi. Just then, she walked in. He had expected her to sleep in, but then again, they had worked up an appetite.

"Good morning, Sam," she said with a smile.

"Good morning, Mimi." He could do this. Bed his wife at night and be friends—at best—during the day.

"How did you sleep?"

"Deeply."

She eyed him curiously but there was no time to finish the conversation as Rudolph walked in. Without standing on ceremony, the man plopped himself down into a chair, not even claiming a morsel of food onto his plate.

The man was a walking irritant. A footman, who undoubtedly had been trained by Rudolph already, piled high a plate of food and placed it before the man.

Rudolph glanced over at Mimi, his gaze lingering significantly longer than Sam would have liked. In fact, if the man didn't take his eyes off his wife—

"I love her." Rudolph proclaimed. "I love her with an undying love."

"What?" How could a man look at a woman and announce his love? Undying or otherwise. It was not possible. The first time Sam had seen Mimi he had not fallen in love. Not even the second time. Third, fourth, and many more. He was not in love with her even though he had taken her innocence and married her. Well, he was as close to love as he was going to get, and it was far enough. Love had no place in his life. He had been forced to concede to a marriage. Not one that he wanted, but one that he could see working out quite nicely for all the parties involved. Namely two. Then again, in the future there would namely be more…and really, that didn't seem so bad. Mimi would make a wonderful mother. And he…well, he might just make a good enough father. Forget that, he would make an excellent father. Whatever he set his mind to, he would do. Or not do. That's just how he was.

"Did you hear me?" Rudolph was shouting now. "I said I love her." His arms were outstretched, pointing toward Mimi.

Hell, no. This man (he couldn't deign to call him his cousin at the moment) had gone too far. It was one thing to threaten his life. It was a completely different thing to threaten to take his woman. Yes, Mimi was his. That was clear. But perhaps not clear enough to Rudolph.

Mimi stood stunned, not moving to the table. Or anywhere.

"I love her." Rudolph shouted again. "You might think I'm crazy, but I shall have her. One way or another." He stood to his feet, and if Sam thought for even a second that Rudolph would lay a hand on Mimi he would call the man ou—

Rudolph lunged toward Mimi. "You, good woman, have shown me the light." He smacked his lips against her cheek and raised his finger into the air. "A wedding! Tomorrow. Or as soon as we can—"

"Over my dead body." Sam was in his cousin's face saying the words he never would have expected to cross his lips. The words his father had spoken far too many times. The words that had led to his father's death. The words that could lead to his own. But there were no greater stakes. "Name your seconds."

— ❧ ❦ ❧ —

CHAPTER TWENTY

"NAME MY SECONDS? What on earth are you talking about?" Rudolph, the weasel, looked befuddled.

"You can't have her," Sam countered, essentially ignoring his cousin's question.

"Why not?"

"You can't possibly love her. You don't even know her."

"*I* don't know her? How can you say that? *You* don't even know her." Rudolph's arms were frantically gesticulating to random spaces in the room, including the area in which Mimi remained standing as still as one of his garden statues that his dog liked to pee on.

Sam was too furious to notice her stillness, and far too beyond rational to see the analogy for what it fully meant.

He was well aware of one thing though. He recognized how little he knew Mimi, but he knew her enough to know she was his and no one was going to take her away from him. Up until this point in time, Rudolph had been a wily weasel, secretive about his effort to take Sam out to try and inherit the dukedom. But of course, just like other men in his family, his cousin was an expressive, impulsive idiot when it came to women. He thought he could take one look at Mimi and claim her? He had another thing coming.

This was beyond the pale. A man couldn't come outright and claim another man's wife.

"I know enough," Sam finally ground out. "And she's mine."

"I don't know what's gotten into you, but whatever reason you think she's yours, you're insane. I cannot, in any conscience, duel a madman."

Sam growled before lunging at Rudolph. The two toppled over, with Sam pinning Rudolph to the ground. He grabbed his cousin's lapels and was shaking the man.

Mimi was now at his side, "Sam, please stop. We'll figure this out."

"This idiot thinks he can make attempts on my life and get away with it. Fine." He throttled Rudolph for good measure. He wanted to make sure his words were sinking in. "But if he thinks for one second he can come in here and take my wife from me—"

"Your wife?" Rudolph shouted.

"Yes, my wife." Sam turned his full attention to his cousin. "If you think you can take her—"

A laugh belted out of Rudolph as he dropped his head to the ground. The laughter rumbled through his body, causing unwelcome vibrations to course through Sam's body.

"What the bloody hell is so funny, you idiot?"

But Rudolph was laughing too hard to answer him. It took a moment for the shaking to cease, and only after Rudolph wiped the teary laughter from his eyes did he finally reply.

"I'm not interested in your wife," he said with a solemn face.

"You said you loved her."

"I do—"

"In my books love screams of interest—"

"I do love her." Rudolph's words were cut off by Sam's growl. "Well, not *her*." He canted his head in Mimi's direction. "I love a woman, who shall remain unnamed for now."

"For God's sake man, why didn't you say that to begin with?" Sam loosened his hold on his cousin, feeling a tidal wave of relief surge over him.

"I thought I did," Rudolph said while rubbing his throat. "At the very least, I never said I loved *her*. I don't even know her."

"My point precisely," Sam grumbled as he stood up. "Get up."

The two men straightened themselves and their attire, and as Sam turned to face Mimi, Rudolph mirrored his actions.

"This is my wife, Mimi."

"Lovely to meet you." Rudolph bowed as if he always acted the perfect gentleman. "And though it pains me to confirm it, I must confess, I do not love you." The man smirked at his feeble attempt at a joke.

"Don't be an arse," Sam grunted at his cousin, pulling his wife into his side.

"Alas, I must admit I am in love. I believe this is a most singular experience in my life." His eyes turned dreamy, and Sam realized that this was the first time he had ever seen his cousin in this way. It was hard to put it into words, but there was no malice in his eyes. No bitterness. Something was missing and had been replaced by love. So the man claimed. Sam was not entirely convinced.

"I'm happy for you and your unnamed woman."

"Thank you." Rudolph shone a large smile at him. "I wanted to share the good news with you before I go and start my new life."

Sam merely acknowledged the man with a nod.

"I shall be off shortly. I have already packed my bags."

And good riddance.

"But…one more thing. What's this about me making attempts on your life?"

Sam shook his head, forgetting that he had disclosed his knowledge of Rudolph's subterfuge.

"Let's forget it, shall we?"

"I would if I could. But I can't…so I won't. You think I've made attempts on your life? Whatever for?"

"Isn't it obvious, Rudolph? Must I really spell it out?"

"I rather think you must."

"You want the dukedom. I understand—"

For the second time in a span of twenty minutes, Rudolph's laughter cut him off. The man was beyond irritating.

"I do not want to take over the dukedom, Sam."

Something about how simple the sentence was and how serious Rudolph sounded made Sam pause. Had he been all wrong about his cousin? Surely not. But…did he actually have proof against Rudolph?

"You don't?"

"No."

"Then why do you show up here?"

"You're my cousin." Rudolph smirked. "And there's this woman nearby, you see…"

"Let me rephrase that. Why do you always show up looking like, acting like, you want to murder me?"

Rudolph stuffed his hands in his pockets. "That is a very good question. I suppose there are a few contributing factors to that, but primarily I always felt as though you didn't want me here." He wasn't wrong about that.

"Are you telling me that this was one giant misunderstanding?"

Mimi interrupted for the first time. "Two giant misunderstandings." She held up her fingers to give more voice to the statement.

"Yes, two misunderstandings."

Rudolph nodded. "It seems that way. But it's a good thing we cleared it up because it looks as though I'll be seeing you much more frequently."

"Why is that?" Sam was afraid to ask.

Mimi nudged him with a smile. "His unnamed woman, I imagine?"

"Ah yes…" Sam said in agreement.

"That is correct. Now, I hate to fight and leave, but I'll see you again soon." Rudolph turned and walked out the door.

"Wonderful," Sam mumbled.

Sam waited for Rudolph to be out of hearing distance and

then said, "I need to take a walk."

"You don't think it's going to rain soon."

"Probably. But it's what I need right now." He raked his hands through his hair. "That, and I need to go see Rex."

"Rex? Who's that?"

"My dog." If he had been thinking more clearly, he would have answered with more kindness in his tone, but at the moment, his brain had turned to pudding and any filters he normally used to screen his thoughts were gone. Hmmm…this must be how Mimi felt every day.

"You have a dog?" He noticed the alarm in her voice and picked up a shred of his decency.

"Yes, I do. But don't worry about Rex. He's been put in a safe place away from you."

"Oh…" she said with her eyes trained on him. "Thank you. That's…very kind of you."

He drew near to her and took her hand in his. "You're my wife, Mimi. I know you have a fear, and I would never subject you to that."

"That's so thoughtful of you, Sam. I don't know what to say."

"There's nothing to say about it. Rex and I will continue our relationship on the side." He winked at her, feeling the need to add some levity to the moment.

"As long as he's your only side thing, I'm all right with it." Her smile made it all worth it. It was no hardship to confine Rex to a large space on the estate and ensure their paths never crossed. It was a small compromise considering the many sacrifices couples had to make.

"I shall go for a walk as well." Her smile warmed his heart.

"That's not necessary, I can take a treat to Rex without you."

"You don't want me to go?"

"I don't want you to do anything you don't want to do. I would never ask you to—"

"You're not asking."

He smiled at her. "That's true."

"And you'll be with me the whole time?"

"I will."

"Then let's go. You can introduce me to Rex." She wrapped her hand around his arm. "I might just wave from a distance, but I'll still say hello. Probably."

"Let's go then."

It was a bit of a walk to find Rex. He was lazing around in a field. Rolling over in the dirt, following butterflies with eyes. Moving about as fast as he normally did, which was the average pace of a turtle. He was an old soul and wasn't the kind to express himself too vividly.

When they reached the fenced off area, Sam placed his hands on the top wrung and looked out at Rex. The dog noticed him but didn't immediately come bounding over, more or less, he looked over his shoulder at Sam and nodded at him. As much as a dog could nod his greeting.

Sam felt his pockets to offer a treat.

"Drat! I forgot his treat. We'll have to go back and get it."

"I think I'll just wait for you."

He raised an eyebrow. "You'll wait here by yourself? With my dog? Alone?"

She lifted her arm to point at the dog, "He hasn't really moved since we got here. And he can't jump the fence, can he?"

Sam laughed as he glanced over at his dog who was now cloud-gazing. "Rex is not the fence-jumping kind."

"I'll be fine."

Sam took off leaving Mimi with Rex.

MIMI COULDN'T REMEMBER the last time she had been alone with a dog. But she couldn't get Sally's words of advice out of her head. Marriage and all its choices. She needed to choose every day who she wanted to be and how she wanted to treat her husband.

Sam was kind enough to separate her from the dog, she could be brave enough to face her fears. Besides, this dog looked harmless. Actually, the dog was practically motionless.

A raindrop landed on the fence. A small drop, but Mimi looked up. She hoped Sam would be returning quickly. She wanted to give Rex his treat and then take shelter.

A few more drops landed, a bit heavier this time. Rex got up. Now that he was on all fours and looking at her, her heart pounded inside of her. Her legs almost trembled, but she scolded them. If Rex had bounded over to them earlier, jumping, barking, and lapping at her, she would have been terrified. There would have been no chance she would have remained alone with him, but he was a slow and quiet dog, keeping to himself.

But with the rain falling, and the clouds growing darker, she could see Rex making his way over to a doghouse. He gave her a look over his shoulder.

Mimi reciprocated the action, looking over her shoulder to see if Sam was in sight yet, but the fields were open behind her.

A loud whimper rang through the air, and she looked back at Rex's enclosed space. She couldn't find him, but she could hear a whimpering sound. As if the dog were hurt.

The rain was beating down now and the air was growing colder. She needed to make a decision quickly.

She could stay where she was and hope Sam would return soon. Then he could find Rex and take care of the dog. That option did not look good. Sam wasn't in sight, and the whimpering sounded awful.

She could run back to the house and get Sam. But that didn't seem very feasible. The rain was almost pouring now. By the time she went home and returned, Rex would be freezing. She couldn't do that to Sam's dog. To Sam.

So the last option she had…the last plan she ever thought she would enact…was the one she chose. She would launch herself over the fence, go find the dog, and comfort him. This dog meant a lot to Sam, and she couldn't have him suffering.

It took all her nerve, all her concentration, and then all of her strength, but she climbed the few feet up the fence and then pushed herself over it. She didn't give her feet a chance to take root, knowing they would if they caught whiff of her fear. Instead, she rushed forward, toward the whimpering sound.

"Rex?" she said in what was hopefully a more calm than frantic voice. "Rex, are you all right? I'm coming."

Another whimper, another step. Then she looked down and saw a hidden ditch in the ground. Rex was lying there whimpering.

"I'm here, Rex." Yes, she was here, but she had no clue what she was going to do. That wasn't true, she knew what she was going to do. She just needed an extra moment to steel her resolve. Finding her backbone, she bent over, putting one foot in the hole, with two arms, she reached around the dog and pulled him to her chest. He was heavier than she expected, but she pushed him up so that he was on level ground. After she pulled herself out of the ditch, she started to walk toward the dog shelter.

Sam's house was too far for her to make the walk with the dog. Rex hobbled behind her. "Come on, boy. Let's get you safe."

It was a slow pace, but thankfully the shelter was only a few yards away. It was huge. Large enough for her to fit inside and wait out the rain with Rex.

Rain beat against the roof while Rex rested his head in her lap. She never thought she would pet a dog again, but Rex wasn't moving.

Gingerly, she brought her hand up to his head and slowly brought it down to pat him. Then she slid her hand down his back.

Never in her wildest fantasies had Mimi ever imagined confining herself into an enclosed area with a dog, waiting to be rescued by her husband.

CHAPTER TWENTY-ONE

WHERE WAS SHE? She was supposed to be waiting by the fence where he left her. From the distance, he could see she wasn't there. Panic ripped through him. The rain was pouring. She was alone with Rex. He trusted the dog, knowing nothing would happen to Mimi, but he couldn't stop envisioning her stiff body back at the house party when that dog had been barreling toward them barking. She was absolutely frozen. How could he be so foolish to leave her alone with Rex? What if she had fainted?

Sam was running now toward the fence, gaining in meters as he approached. "Mimi!" His shouts were lost through the downpour. "Mimi!" He tried again. His vision was blurry and his heart was a mess. He couldn't see Rex either now. Where the deuce had they gone? And together?

He trudged around the fence and then hopped over the fence. There was no way Rex escaped, was there? But what would have prompted Mimi to enter? Or had she returned to the house? Impossible. He would have seen her. And she wouldn't have taken off in a different direction with the imminent rain clouds.

He couldn't imagine the two together. But if Rex were alone, he probably would have taken shelter in his doghouse. Perhaps Rex could help him find Mimi. Sam jaunted over to the doghouse and bent down. To his utter disbelief, he saw Rex curled around Mimi with his head in her lap while she stroked his head.

"Mimi, are you all right?"

She had tears down her cheeks, but she didn't appear to be afraid. "He got hurt. I-I had to help him. He was stuck and whimpering."

At this point, Sam was crouching as far as he could into the small space, his head ducked under the shelter. His heart felt inflated, full. Overflowing. This woman.

"Mimi," he leaned in and brushed a hand across her cheek. "You must have been terrified. Why did you do it?"

"He's your dog. You love him. I had to help him." Her voice was trembling yet still strong. Because she was strong. She was brave. To face her fears, her paralyzing fears, for him. Her courage was inspiring. Humbling. Captivating.

"My God, Mimi. I love the dog, but I—" He stopped himself. He knew what he was going to say, and his lips were shocked into silence. How long had his heart known how it felt? At what point had it made up its mind? And why had it taken so long to send the message to his head? She had always been so vexing to him, was that only because he thought he couldn't have her? Shouldn't have her? He never trusted himself to love someone until her. It had all happened so fast, one minute he thought her irritating, and the next she had been irresistible. There was no turning back. She was beyond incredible.

"What?" Her lips parted, and he wanted to kiss her.

"I love you more."

"You do?" The hope in her eyes told him what he hadn't acknowledged, but what he had longed to know. He was desperate to know how she felt about him.

"I do." He reached in and pulled her out of the doghouse. He swept her up into his arms and spun around, nuzzling his lips into her hair as the rain dripped down on them. This woman was the most fearless, most beautiful, most lovable hellion he had ever known. Acting his most reckless, he had almost dueled over her. But that was because he thought he could lose her.

There was no way he would ever lose her. He would love her

senseless before that ever happened.

"I should have done this earlier," he mumbled into her neck.

"What? Tell me you love me?"

"If I had known that earlier, I would have told you. But I also mean this," he spun around again, "hold you in my arms, spinning you around. When you won the tournament. I should have celebrated you more. I will celebrate you every day for the rest of our lives."

She leaned in and kissed his mouth. Pure delight soaked through him.

"I can't believe you love me."

"I can't believe it either. But I do." He smiled at the love of his life. His forever.

"I almost trapped you as part of the duke dare, but I knew I couldn't do that to you," Mimi said with her hand on his chest.

"What duke dare?"

"The one my sisters and I agreed to. We would each find a duke this season to marry."

"Well, you found one, and technically you did trap me."

"Not intentionally." He could see the honesty in her eyes, and he loved her more for it. She was not the kind to be manipulative.

"That's good to know. It makes a difference."

"It makes all the difference in the world. I would never do that to you, Sam. You're a good man. One of the best, in fact."

His feelings felt like clotted cream. She thought he was a good man? One of the best?

Then again, that's what Mimi did. By being the best version of herself, she called out others to be better. If they answered the call, they would rise with her. Just like in the archery tournament. She didn't let up. Even though she was a lady, and it was expected of her to be meek. No one would have faulted her if she missed the target altogether and giggled away her actions. But no, not Mimi. She stood tall, focused, determined to win. And then she did. She gave her all, and bested them all.

And when they danced in the rain, yes many guests had run

inside, but several had turned back and stayed outside and danced with them. Each savoring the moment. Because of her.

By being her best self, others became better.

That's what she was doing to him.

"And how do you feel about me, Mimi?"

"I love you, Sam." Whenever Mimi spoke quietly like that, it reverberated through his bones, as though he felt the words and didn't just hear them.

"If you love me, you would be dramatic about it. You would shout it at the top of your lungs."

She grinned, dropped her head back and shouted into the rain, "I love you!"

Not to be out done, he bellowed, "I love you more!"

And perhaps they would have stayed and danced in the rain again, this time knowingly in love, but a soft bark sounded from the doghouse, causing them both to laugh.

"I'll grab Rex. Then we can run inside and warm up."

"The race is on," Mimi shouted playfully. And he had never felt so light. So happy. Playful and competitive. Passionate.

He grabbed Rex, doing a quick check on his injury, and then turned to chase after Mimi toward the house.

The rain was still dripping but the sun had come out while they laughed their way inside. Sam gave Rex a quick kiss and handed him to Bixly, the butler. "Call the veterinarian. He looks all right now, but Mimi said he got hurt. I'll check in on him shortly."

Mimi was ahead of him, going up to their room, dropping wet clothes all the way up the stairs. With each layer removed, he grew desperate to take his lover into his arms.

Thankfully the onlookers (namely a footman or two, Bixly, and her lady's maid) only stifled their chuckles at the sight of him chasing after Mimi. They had always been loyal and kind. He was good to them, and they had always been good to him.

"Mimi," he called out just before entering their room. "You had better be naked by the time I close this door—" He didn't even need to finish his sentence. She stood in all her curves by the fire. Hair dripping wet down her shoulders. Breasts perked up to see him. And her hands on her thighs, where he could already imagine how wet she would be.

"God, you're the most amazing woman I've ever met."

"Is that so?" she teased him.

He nodded slowly, advancing toward her while peeling off his own layers.

"Are you just saying that because I'm the better archer?"

"Mostly," he smirked at her, now naked from the waist up.

"Well, you're pretty amazing as well," she said with a twinkle in her eyes.

"Are you just saying that because I beat you in an arm wrestle?"

A velvety laugh erupted from her and she ran toward him. He picked her up and she wrapped her legs around his waist.

"Let's agree that we're both amazing." She dipped her eyes to his lips.

"Agreed." He claimed her mouth with his.

Within a few steps he had her near the fire to get them dry and warm. "I'm going to lay you on the floor and make love to you, Mimi."

"I want you to take me everywhere." She reclined back on her elbows, propping her bosom up and on display. Her knees were up, gathered to a point.

"Spread your legs for me," he instructed in a husky voice.

Gradually, she released the hold her knees had on each other and slowly parted her legs. Her eyes remained steady on him as he dropped his breeches.

She gasped at the sight of his cock and licked her lips. When he laid down on his stomach, head between her thighs, he whispered, "Don't move, my love."

Beyond words, she hummed her acquiescence. With soft movements, he parted her slit and unleashed his tongue on her sweet nectar. "Mimi, you're my favorite dessert."

Her head had dropped back, and her mouth was parted. With each lick, each press, each suckle, her breaths grew shorter and shallower.

"Sam," she whimpered.

"That wasn't loud enough Mimi."

Her only response was a soft mewl.

"I know you can be louder than that." He licked her slowly all along her seam. "I'll do this all night if I have to, but I won't stop until you're screaming my name."

"Uhh…" A throaty moan broke free.

He flicked his tongue over her pearl. Back and forth. Back and forth. Until her thighs were attempting to squeeze around his head. He used his arms to hold her down and started to suck on her nub.

Her body trembled, and she shouted his name. When her legs went limp, he climbed up over her. Gently, he held her strong and released her elbows from underneath her, then laid her head on the ground.

"Are you ready for me, my love?"

Biting her bottom lip, she said, "Yes, Sam. I want you inside of me. I need you to fill me up." She arched her hips up against his cock, sliding down his hard ridge.

"We can go slow later, but for now, I need you." He wanted to watch her. "I want to feel you come all along my cock. I'm going to coat you inside and own you."

"You already do. I'm yours."

"And I'm yours, Mimi."

"Mmm…" She smiled warmly and pulled her leg over his hip. He grabbed her leg and put it over his shoulder instead.

When he slid his cock into her, he groaned at the heat. The comfort. The peace. This was home. This was everything. She was everything to him. "That's the slowest I can go, my love."

"I don't need slow. I just need you."

He thrust into her, moving her up the rug. "Hold onto me."

She reached up and tangled her hands into his hair. And he

thrust into her again all the way to the hilt. Bottoming out, his sack grew tight. A tingle flared up his spine and his legs began to tremble.

Mimi was more than he could have ever dreamed. He had never felt this captivated before. She was clenched around him, not letting go. She could suck him dry and fill his cup at the same time. Theirs would be a relationship for the ages. Loving. Competing. Filling. Completing each other.

Her hands were all over him, exploring, gripping. He kissed her, with their tongues clashing, devouring each other. He couldn't get enough.

The sensations were overwhelming and building. He could feel himself about to explode, but he wanted to hang on to please her one more time.

"Sam!" she shouted, sitting up, clinging to his shoulders. "Uhhh…yes…Sam!" He thrust into her again, hitting that spot in hopes she would wring him dry. Her insides clenched around him, shuddering. He thrust one more time. Another scream, a whimper. Her head was resting against his shoulder. She was sucking on his neck.

And then he felt that last fearless squeeze and he let himself go. He grunted and held her firmly against his body. He would never let her go. Ever.

$$-\ \text{《《◎》◎◎◎》}\ -$$

EPILOGUE

"I'M STILL SHOCKED that we got married before Joan and James," Mimi said, stroking Sam's hair. There was no fantasy that could beat this. The most handsome man she had ever met was wrapped around her, physically, emotionally, spiritually. She knew him better than anyone else, and she loved him. More than that, he knew her fully and loved her.

He had hauled her off in his arms more times than should be allowed in one lifetime, and he had truly swept her off her feet, starting right after she had rescued Rex. Best choice she ever made.

But facing her fears had always been her best choice, she just never knew the depths of fears she would have to face. With each choice she made, she knew it was right. It was always right to choose love over fear. Fear locked a person down while love freed a person up.

"I'm still shocked that it only took one day for Rex to like you better than he likes me." He wrapped his hand around her thigh and stroked her. "He's a traitor."

"Of course he likes me better. I saved his life."

"I wouldn't go that far."

She swatted his shoulder as he conceded, "All right, you saved his life. He did have a limp for a day."

"Thank God he's all right now."

"After seeing you with that first dog, I never would have

thought you would overcome your fears so quickly."

"Oh, I haven't completely overcome my fears. But I love Rex. He's the best dog in the whole world."

"Of course he is. He's mine."

Mimi laughed. "That must be it." She placed a soft kiss on his cheek. "When are we going to have that rematch on the arm wrestle?"

"I didn't think that was something we were ever going to do."

Mimi sat up, pushing his hand off of her. "Of course it's something we're going to do. I've been practicing."

"With who?"

"Bixly."

"What?"

She burst out laughing. "I was just—"

"Very funny, duchess."

He rolled over her naked frame, their bodies pressing together. "You must think you're so funny."

"I do, indeed."

He covered her mouth with a kiss.

"I could get used to this. Kisses from you. Naked days." She wiggled her brows at him.

"I won't have it any other way."

And they spent the rest of the day in bed, making love.

Oh, and there may have even been a second arm wrestle, but it's unclear who won that one.

About the Author

Eliana Piers, award-winning and international best-selling author, has been writing and singing stories since she was five years old. After feeling inspired by authors like Julia Quinn, Tessa Dare, and Minerva Spencer, Eliana decided to test her quill on the page.

Writing about love and how two people come to connect and share parts of their souls with each other is now an obsession.

It's not worth it if you don't laugh, learn, or love while you're in it.

Eliana lives in Canada where she drinks an iced cap every day.

9 781967 169832